THE MIGRATION OF GHOSTS

THE MIGRATION

OF GHOSTS

Pauline Melville

BLOOMSBURY

'The President's Exile' first appeared in *New Writing 6*,
Eds. A.S. Byatt and Peter Porter (Vintage in association
with the British Council, 1997)

Published by Bloomsbury Publishing, New York and London.
Distributed to the trade by St. Martin's Press

A CIP catalogue record for this book
is available from the Library of Congress

ISBN 1-58234-020-X

First published in Great Britain 1998
by Bloomsbury Publishing Plc

First U.S. Edition 1999
10 9 8 7 6 5 4 3 2 1

Typeset in Scotland by Hewer Text Ltd, Edinburgh
Printed in the United States of America by
R.R. Donnelley & Sons Company, Harrisonburg, Virginia

FOR JOY

And let thy goste thee lede
– 'Balade de Bone Conseyl', Chaucer

CONTENTS

THE
PRESIDENT'S
EXILE

The president walked up the steps to the entrance of the London School of Economics where he had studied as a young man. He wore a calf-length, navy-blue alpaca coat and a fawn cashmere scarf tied neatly, like a cravat, around his neck. Recently he had undergone an operation on his throat and he worried about protecting the vulnerable area from the cold winds of a London winter.

He passed through the swing doors and stood for a moment on the marbled floor of the large entrance hall. It was not term-time and there were few people about. Nobody recognised him. He remained there for a minute or two. The balding man at the porter's desk was looking down at some list or other and paid him no attention. He hesitated for a moment wondering what he should say if asked what he was doing there. He would simply say that he was President Hercules and that he had studied law here some thirty – or, goodness, was it forty – years previously and that he had now returned to take an affectionate walk around the place.

In fact, he had not been happy there. Nobody would recognise him, he knew that. It was too long ago. Nor would they know that he was in exile.

His hand gripped the bottom of the briefcase under his arm more tightly at the recollection of his new and unaccustomed lack of status. It was still unclear to him how it had happened. However hard he tried to remember, the precise sequence of events escaped him. The transition from real president to exiled president remained a blur. The more he sat in his hotel room and tried to remember, the more it slipped from his grasp. He wondered whether he might not be in the throes of a nervous breakdown.

He remembered entering the hospital for minor throat surgery. The limousine had delivered him to the front doors where a team of Cuban doctors waited to greet him. The sun was blazing down. He remembered the warm wind on his cheeks. Photographers took pictures of him shaking hands with the surgeons before going inside. After that, he remembered nothing.

The president was standing staring at the floor when he realised that by remaining motionless he would attract attention. He walked over to the lift. Inside he randomly pressed a button. He could not remember which floor housed the law faculty and anyway it had probably all changed. But stepping out of the lift on the third floor, he felt a familiar sense of unease as he recognised the shabby corridors and the warm smell of dull, wooden doors and cheap furniture polish. Notices on various offices indicated that this was now the social anthropology department. But it was certainly the same floor that had once housed the department of legal studies.

He looked through the small window in the door of one of the rooms, cupping his hand to shade his eyes from the reflection. The long, solid desks were the same ones he remembered but now each desk supported a row of grey computers. He tried the door. It was locked. He stared through the window.

Why had he felt drawn to visit this place again? There had, after all, been enough successes in his life. Why, he wondered, should he feel compelled to return to where he had suffered an unforgettable, if minor, humiliation. He recalled the episode.

His tutor had waved his essay in front of the rest of the seminar group and then handed it back to him with the words:

'This is remarkably like an essay from one of the current third-year students that I marked last year. I shall give you the benefit of the doubt this time but I warn you that if anything similar occurs again I shall report it to the dean.'

Naturally, he had feigned surprise and looked mystified, although he had, in fact, copied the essay from the student whose effort had been marked with an alpha plus. His own work was of a reasonably high standard but it was the certainty of obtaining the best grade that he had been unable to resist.

That same evening, a group of colonial students at the Mecklenberg Square hostel listened and sympathised as he insisted with righteous indignation, over the evening meal of chops and gravy, that the similarity between the essays had been an extraordinary and unfortunate coincidence. He talked scathingly of his tutor whom, he said, undoubtedly shared the racial bias common to all colonial masters and just wanted to see him degraded.

Several of the students from that batch at Mecklenberg Square had gone on to do well in later life. Two were currently prime ministers of African states. One had gone

to Sandhurst Military Academy and was now a general in
Ghana. He himself had become the first black president in
South America.

He prided himself on the fact that he was one of the
few presidents on that continent who could mix and feel
at ease with the crowd in the marketplace. Sometimes he
would order his driver to stop the car at one of the street
markets so that he could walk amongst the pungent smells of
vegetables, herbs, washing powders and cocoa beans or stroll
between the stiff carcasses of dried fish, to talk and joke with
the stall-holders and ask them about business. In his speeches
he often referred to the importance of 'the small man'.

It was the same on open days at his official residence. He
enjoyed the *bonhomie*, mingling with people in the grounds,
chatting, gesticulating and jostling his way through the guests as
those around him closed in and clapped him on the back.

But when he was out of the country, officiating as head of
state at some international conference and he bumped into
his former fellow students, he fretted over whether any of
them remembered the time that he was accused of cheating
and the public smile froze on his face.

The odd thing was that even after he had been president
for many years, he felt unsure of his position. He felt like
a charlatan. And this was nothing to do with the rigged
elections that had kept him in power for nearly two decades.
He would have felt like a charlatan even if he had been fairly
elected.

His father, a civil servant, had once told him he would
never amount to anything because he lacked moral fibre. The
office of president felt like a carapace he had assumed to cover
his failings. The only question he ever really wanted to ask his

fellow presidents and prime ministers at those conferences was whether they felt the same.

'Do you feel too that we're all a bunch of frauds?' he wanted to ask, but never did.

He turned away from the seminar room and walked down the corridor back towards the lift. He inspected his Cartier watch. Quarter-past eleven. He had nowhere particular to go and for some reason felt reluctant to leave the building straight away.

He abandoned the lift on the ground floor and made his way to the Old Theatre. This was where important visiting lecturers delivered their addresses. Nobody paid heed to him and he walked over to the door on the right and slipped quietly inside.

Here things had changed. The auditorium was at the same raked angle as he remembered but instead of the parquet flooring and banks of gloomy, high-backed, oak seats, the entire place had been carpeted and the wooden benches replaced by plush and comfortable seats like a real theatre.

There was no one there. A microphone stand, an empty glass and dusty jug of water stood on a table on the stage awaiting some phantom speaker. The president sank into one of the upholstered chairs with relief and put his briefcase down on the seat next to him. He loosened the scarf round his neck gingerly. The operation wound on his throat had not healed properly. Sometimes it oozed a colourless fluid. He touched the ridged scar gently with his fingertips. They came away a little wet. He searched for a handkerchief in his coat pocket and held it against the places where the seeping plasma escaped.

Anxious to put out of his mind the unpleasant memories

occasioned by his visit upstairs, he tried to console himself by re-living the time when he had won the Best Speaker's Prize for oratory at the Inns of Court. But all he could remember was how he had felt at the time – a sense of incredulity that the judges should reward him for something that was so easy, telling lies in a powerful and persuasive manner. He could barely see the credit in that because even as a child he had recognised the distinction between public lies and private truths. He thought it was second nature to everyone. What was oratory if not the art of public lies? For him, all discourse was to some extent a matter of lying.

Lying had never been a problem. It is easy for those with a good grasp of reality. The same sound grasp of reality made him a pragmatic politician.

'It is simple,' he had said in the early days of his political life. 'I am the African leader. My rival is the East Indian leader.' He would say this quite openly when most of the progressive forces in the fifties supported his rival whom they understood to be leader of the masses. His rival campaigned up and down the country on the basis of racial unity. Meanwhile, he negotiated with the Americans and British and took power knowing he would be able to rely on people to vote on the basis of racial division.

'I deal with realities,' he said.

And it was this that made his present position so disturbing. He was not sure exactly what the reality was. If he knew the events that had led him here, he would know what to do about his current situation. But he seemed to have difficulty in concentrating. He leaned forward in his seat and clenched his fists together, head between his hands. The important matters were vague, yet other irritating and inconsequential memories such as the tutor accusing him of cheating all those years ago remained vividly in his mind.

Feeling a little hot, he opened the top buttons of his coat. For some reason his thoughts travelled back to the occasion when his father had compared him unfavourably to one of his schoolfriends, a certain Michael Yates. He was eleven. He had arrived home from school to find his father standing on the polished floor in front of the open verandah doors, scowling over a letter from his headmaster. It concerned some minor misdemeanour. It was not the misdemeanour that the headmaster complained of, however, but the disproportionate and elaborate web of lies and deception that had been fabricated to cover it up.

'You shame me,' his father had roared while his sister looked on with satisfaction from beside the dresser. 'Why you can't be like Michael Yates? Michael Yates is open and honest. Michael Yates is a straightforward boy. You sneaky. Why do I have to have a lampey-pampey sneak for a son?'

Years later, as president, when he was about to make a speech at the Critchlow Labour College, he spotted a familiar figure as he made his way down the aisle to the rostrum. These were the days when he had begun to wear an item of purple every day and to sign his name in purple ink like an emperor. He stopped to shake the hand of his old friend from schooldays, whose hair was now thinning on either side of a peak at the front and who beamed at him from the sidelines.

'Michael Yates. What are you up to these days?'

'I'm teaching in the secondary school at West Ruimveldt.'

The president slapped him on the back.

'Pleased to hear it,' he said, before continuing down to the platform.

That afternoon, the president arrived back at his office and told his secretary to ensure forthwith that a Mr Michael Yates was sacked from his post at West Ruimveldt secondary school and refused a post anywhere else. For the rest of the morning he basked in the satisfaction of an ancient score settled. President Hercules had a phenomenal memory for slights. He could remember any politician who had offended or opposed him and the precise details of the occasion.

A cleaner bumped the doors of the theatre open with her behind and entered backwards dragging a hoover. The president gathered up his belongings and edged between the rows of seats towards the exit.

He found himself in Kingsway. He looked briefly for a restaurant he used to frequent but it was no longer there. It had been replaced by a print and graphics store.

The traffic streamed past him down towards Bush House. In a gap between two buildings opposite stood a beech tree, its delicate branches traced like a frozen neurone against the blank January sky. Missing the heat and humidity of his own country, he turned and walked in the other direction, away from Kingsway, down the Strand.

There was no doubt that this exile was a temporary state of affairs. He would return eventually. When, was the question. He turned into Northumberland Avenue.

The heavy, revolving doors of the building that housed the Royal Commonwealth Society decanted him slowly through and he was relieved to feel the burst of warmth as he entered. A uniformed security official trod silently across a sea of red carpet, presumably to ask him his business. President Hercules took the man by the elbow across to where a photographic portrait of the Queen and the Commonwealth heads of state hung on the wall. He pointed out his own picture in the line-up and laughed off the man's embarrassment, tapping him lightly on the back to show that no offence was taken.

The security man looked confused and apologetic as he returned to his position. The president took the lift to the first floor. He seemed bound by a compulsion to return to the scenes of episodes in his life which had shamed or demeaned him in some way. He could not stay away. It was as if, by returning and concentrating with all his energy on these episodes, he might be able to expunge them from history. And yet they were all minor setbacks compared to his achievements. Why did his achievements mean nothing?

In the lift he began to sweat as he remembered in detail what had happened there.

The incident had taken place when he had already been prime minister for several years and had just appointed himself president for life. He had stopped off in London on his return journey from the Commonwealth Conference in Lagos. The meeting he had chosen to address was not a public one but one by private invitation only. He must have had something of a premonition because he had left specific instructions that his sister was not to be invited. On his accession to the presidency, he had cancelled her diplomatic post in an act of private spite after she refused him a small piece of sculpture that their father had left her in his will. She had remained in London and he knew that his action still rankled with her. He did not want to see her in public lest she caused a fuss about it.

His sister, however, had persuaded a friend to bring her along as a guest. The president was relaxed and in good form. He wore an immaculate khaki shirt-jack that sloped gently out from his chest to accommodate the foothills of what was later to become a mountainous waist.

As his speech finished to a round of applause, he stepped forward to shake hands, first with the High Commissioner, then with other selected dignitaries and party supporters. At that precise moment, his sister stepped out of the lift into the foyer on the first floor where the small but distinguished audience milled about holding glasses of wine and chatting.

'I will probably get into trouble for this, but I should like you all to know certain things about my brother, Baldwin Hercules.' She spoke in an uncertain voice, but her feet were planted firmly apart and she held her handbag in both trembling hands.

The gathering grew uneasily silent as she stood nervously in front of the lift doors, her head thrown back a little. She continued determinedly, looking straight into the eyes of her audience.

'Nobody knows a man better than his own sister. Baldwin is a liar, a cheat and a bully. As a child, he always lied his way out of trouble. Lied. Lied. Lied. He always had to blame somebody else. He wanted to win everything. Yes, he is clever, but he has a cruel streak. And I am warning you. You have let him have too much power. You all will suffer for it and so will the country. There is nothing he will not do and nobody he will not use to get what he wants.'

A couple of people moved forwards to try and persuade her gently to leave. One of them pressed the button to open the lift doors behind her. Nothing happened. The lift had stuck. She continued, speaking more quickly now because she sensed that his security guards might bundle her out.

'Somebody has to speak the truth before it is too late. We all know that elections are rigged. We must be the only country where the government is elected by the dead. Half the names on the lists are taken from tombstones. Eventually, he will kill to stay where he is. Socialist republic?' She sneered. 'Ask him why his daughter had to take up residence in Switzerland. I will tell you why – to caretake his secret bank accounts.'

She turned her troubled eyes to the friend who had brought her there as a guest.

'I'm sorry,' she said. 'I shouldn't have done this. But I couldn't help it.' And she turned away from the lift and walked in silence down the carpeted stairs.

That night she took a flight to Canada.

During most of her outburst the president stood silent, an embarrassed smile on his face, his cheeks crawling with horror. When she mentioned the Swiss bank accounts, he turned away and began to speak with an air of amused resignation to one of his entourage.

'A pity you can't sack your family in the same way you can sack your ministers,' he said ruefully, attempting to laugh the whole thing off. Sweat glistened in the creases of his neck. The man he addressed responded with a bray of palpably false laughter.

Now the exiled president walked softly to the place where he had stood all those years ago. He stood in exactly the same spot on the carpet as if he were once again facing his sister, surrounded by phantom dignitaries. Prickles ran up his neck and along his jaw. He rubbed the thumb of his right hand against the middle finger nervously. He could hear once again every word she said and he shuddered as though his soul were being branded.

He had never taken retaliatory action against his sister for the simple reason that he never thought he could get away with it. She lived in Canada. If she had returned to her own country it would have been different. She would have been within his orbit.

Standing there in those gracious surroundings, he recalled the successful assassination of one of his political opponents. The man was a popular radical who posed him a considerable threat. He recollected the man's death with perfect equanimity and with a sense of satisfaction. He had no reservations about the use of power. Power must be used ruthlessly to be effective. He had never suffered a moment's regret about the murder. In fact, he considered it to be one of his most subtle triumphs.

The assassination had pleased him because there had been no need for him to do more than express a desire that the man did not exist. He had flung a newspaper down on the table at a ministerial meeting, groaned with mock theatricality and wished out loud that the radical could be stopped from holding these mass meetings at which he made inflammatory statements. Although it was not the meetings that had infuriated him. It was the fact that the young man had referred to him in public as King Kong. He then scribbled down a list of eleven names of those he considered to be potentially dangerous. The revolutionary's name headed the list.

'Here is a cricket team that is not batting on our side.' He had looked around the circle of watchful eyes and shrugged with exaggerated regret. 'The captain is one I could do without.'

A few weeks later, the man was blown apart in his own car

and he, the president, had been able to say, with his hand on his heart, that he knew nothing about it. Although it irritated him to find out that, in a fit of overzealousness, one of his ministers had issued a statement to the press disclaiming all responsibility for the death before it had actually occurred.

By that time, of course, his henchmen knew how to fulfil his slightest whim. His diet, for instance. He began the day by drinking half a beer mug of orange juice with two raw eggs cracked in it, whisked around with port wine to form a greyish-purple liquid. It was a longevity diet. Occasionally, he swallowed a turtle's heart while it was still beating so that he could absorb the power of life.

Remembering his opponent's violent demise raised his spirits a little. The knowledge that he had got away with it afforded him some relief from the burning and shameful memory of his sister's denunciation. He pulled up his coat collar, making sure his throat was well protected from the icy weather, then walked slowly down the stairs and nodded politely to the attendant before shouldering his way through the revolving doors and out into the cold once more.

This time he took a bus to the High Commission. He wanted to find out whether his portrait was still hanging there. He screwed up his face a little. Something about those airbrushed official portraits always made him look a little prissy – the cheeks too plump; the thin moustache resting on his full top lip and short, greying beard on the point of his chin gave him the somewhat pampered look of a man both smug and guarded, possibly a little shy. But it would reassure him to see the picture still hanging there on the wall. He would take one more look before returning to his hotel.

13

He walked past the red-brick, bay-windowed building several times. The portrait was gone. It was no longer there. His stomach muscles tightened with anxiety. As he watched they were replacing it with his successor. The solemn face of his deputy prime minister, bumbling Edwin Jeffson, was being hoisted into position.

He stood in a daze in the street. A small cockney boy, his face marbled with cold, ran past the railings twanging them with a stick. The noise brought him to his senses. There was nothing to do but return immediately to his hotel. He still suffered fits of dizziness. Clearly, he was not fully recovered from the operation. He should go and lie down and try to work out how to return as quickly as possible before his position became irreversible.

The functional anonymity of the hotel room helped settle his jangled nerves. He lay down stiffly on the bed without removing his overcoat. The trouble was, these patches of fog in his mind. He wondered if they were some unforeseen side-effect of the operation. He could remember more or less everything up until then.

For a moment he wondered whether Castro had sent a team of doctors to incapacitate him as part of some take-over bid. Unlikely. And if that were the case, why was the portrait of his deputy prime minister, Edwin Jeffson, hanging in the High Commission? Jeffson was a born subordinate. He could not imagine Jeffson being behind any plot to oust him. That was why he had appointed him as his deputy.

Wrack his brains as he might, he had no idea how he had arrived in London. Could he have been drugged?

Perhaps he had done something terrible when he was still under the influence of the anaesthetic – made a fool of himself in some way and been discreetly removed for a while. A military take-over was unlikely. The generals and brigadiers were in his pocket. Although, of course, you could never be certain. What kept troubling him was the idea that he might have suffered some kind of mental breakdown.

He frowned. Suddenly he had remembered his horse. He hoped Jason the groom would care for it properly in his absence. He loved to ride his great white steed arrayed in the splendid leather saddle and harness presented to him by President Lyndon Johnson of the United States. Villagers became used to the sight of him walking the horse between Belfield and Golden Grove. His favourite official portrait showed him mounted in the saddle.

One thing he did know for sure. He should return soon. It would not be wise to wait for too long. He did not want Edwin Jeffson to become accustomed to the trappings of office.

Some stains on the scarf that lay beside him on the bed caught his attention. He put his hand to his neck. When he inspected his fingers, he saw that the fluid was a pale pink colour as if there were traces of blood in it. He went into the bathroom, but dazzled by the white tiles and brilliant lights he became suddenly fearful of looking at the wound in the mirror. He stepped hastily back into his room.

Before he slept, he worried briefly about running out of money. But there was always his watch and the gold signet ring. Back home he had encouraged people to kneel and kiss this ring, pretending always that it was a huge joke, but not liking it when people demurred. He could always ask for money to be telegraphed through to him from his Swiss account.

The next morning, he decided to brave the icy drizzle and do something that his official position had never allowed him to do before. He decided to visit Madame Tussaud's. The idea of a hall of notoriety for both the famous and the infamous had always fascinated him. On arrival, he had no choice but to queue in the freezing sleet along with the other visitors in the Marylebone Road. When he came out two hours later, in contrast to the eminent waxworks, secure and almost complacent in their fixed history, he was overcome by anxiety and paced up and down the Inner Circle of Regent's Park, going nowhere. It was then he decided that he would return to his own country the next day, secretly, via Surinam.

In his homeland, the president's official residence had remained empty since his departure, but the lights were still left on there at night to allay the fears of the populace. The attractive, rambling building stood in its own grounds, surrounded by royal palms, and clearly visible from the road.

The house was uninhabited. Maids and cleaners attended to their duties as infrequently as possible. Nobody wanted to go there. Even relatives had gone in only briefly to collect their belongings and scurry away.

There were reports that his white horse had been heard moving slowly about in the spacious galleries upstairs. Nobody was sure he was gone for good. The story also gained ground that a black cayman had been seen slithering down the front steps of the residence. On reaching the ground, the creature had stood up in the shape of a man. To cap it all, one of the ex-maids had apparently started to speak with the president's voice.

A storekeeper from the village of Vigilance recounted his dream to anyone who would listen:

'One day I was walking out on to the street. Gradually, I notice many people standing on either side of the road in small groups and knots, kind of muttering and whispering amongst themselves. As I proceeded, the groups became silent and everybody stood looking backwards down the road towards Belfield. A hearse was coming down the road. President Hercules was sitting in it. He shouted out to a man on the roadside in his usual, loudmouth way, "That business with the house – it fix?"

'The man said no.

"Stop by my house tomorrow. I see to it."

'And suddenly the hearse jerked and veered to the left.' The storekeeper leaned over the counter to his customers. 'A burial place should be near a fork in the road, you know, so that the funeral party can make a sudden turn and confuse the spirits. So the African legend goes.' The dream had so impressed him that he continued telling it to each new customer.

'Then I dreamed I found myself near a small church. A priest stood with a baby in his arms as if for a christening. The baby had the face of an old man – sinister. Gradually, I see who the face belong to. It belong to Hercules. I asked my uncle what music was playing.

"The Dead March", replied my uncle.

'And then, you know how it is with dreams, I was at home once more in Vigilance looking out of the window. The whole area was flooded for as far as I could see. The water reached right up to the top windows. Then it began to ebb and recede like mist until it was gone.'

The whole country abounded with rumours and hearsay.

There were rumours that President Hercules had been seen in Moscow, in the United States, and now it was even being said that he had been seen standing amongst the waxworks at Madame Tussaud's.

It was at just this time, when such rumours were at their height, that the president contrived to return incognito. The whole operation was clandestine. He wanted to get back into his own country secretly and assess the situation. It was best to stay out of the capital where his face was too well known. He would spend time in the interior where there would be less chance of his being recognised.

It was a warm, voluptuous night when the president once again felt the soil of his own land under his feet.

The first night of his return he stayed in a disused hut on an abandoned trail outside Orealla. For most of the night he sat in the pitch dark, on a rough wooden plank, planning what to do. Every so often he fingered his neck gingerly. All night long his ring finger itched and he worried that he was developing a nervous allergy.

It would have been more sensible to travel at night when there was less chance of recognition but he was not accustomed to the bush and feared losing himself. Transportation was clearly going to pose a problem. Regretfully, he decided he must risk going into the capital to fetch his horse.

Early the next morning, he set off. A storm helped him. He took a lift in a donkey cart. The tropical deluge turned the air grey and allowed him to pull the hood of his green military cape down so that it nearly covered his face. Worst of all was the fear that he had begun to smell. He had not been able to wash properly since leaving England and in this climate, he feared that the wound in his neck would become putrid.

By nightfall of the next evening he had reached the outskirts of the city.

It was a clear night. The presidential mansion was open, unguarded and with the lights blazing as usual from the deserted rooms. He walked down the path, through the door and up the steps directly facing him. It was just as he had last seen it except that all signs of his occupancy, his personal belongings and effects had been removed. He walked through every room, his footsteps making a hollow echo on the shiny wooden floors, polished to translucence. He breathed deeply. Then he went out and stood for a while on the verandah, looking out towards the statue of a heroic slave leader who had led a rebellion in the eighteenth century.

He could just make out the figure of the statue. Even in the dark there was something bleak about the empty, treeless space surrounding it. In the daytime, traffic swirled round the plinth at a distance. Few people went close up to it. Some said that it possessed a force that pushed people away. Others said that the statue had an intimate connection with the president through magical and arcane writings on the back of its head and that they would never be sure that the president had gone for good until the statue fell.

For a while, he looked out over the city and brooded on what to do next.

As he stepped back inside, a violent snuffling, snorting noise from the next room startled him. He tiptoed along the verandah back to the main reception room.

Standing there, head lowered, eyes looking at him, was his white horse. He rushed over to greet it, grasping it by the mane and burying his head it the animal's neck. He ran his hand down the horse's flanks. They felt hot and sweaty as though it had recently been ridden. He cursed the groom for not attending properly to the animal which was still steaming with heat. It had not even been unsaddled. On its back sat the magnificent, tooled leather saddle donated by the United States of America and normally used only on state occasions. The president hurried into the next room to see if there was any sign of his purple riding boots. No trace of them. He came thoughtfully back to where the horse waited.

And then, President Hercules mounted his horse. His head reached nearly to the crystal chandelier. The tops of the landscapes and portraits hanging on the walls came level with his shoulders. He moved the horse slowly through the room and after a little persuasion, the white charger edged itself sideways and awkwardly, with clattering hooves, descended the main stairway.

Horse and rider walked through the main doors of the house, down the path, past the unoccupied guard-hut on the left, past the ghostly trunks of the giant royal palms and out into the sleeping city.

He could not resist it. It was three o'clock in the morning. He took a tour. The city was deserted. He rode past the parliament building. There was a slight drizzle and a chill bite to the air.

'Cold. Cold,' he said to himself. 'Ice-cart coming.'

He cantered on through the empty streets, the horse's hooves throwing up spray from the waterlogged ground. For nostalgia's sake, he took the road past one particular house. It was one of the enormous old colonial, white wooden houses. The Demerara shutters opened on to the night. Once his father had taken him to this house, explaining that it represented the soul of the country and all that was good in it. He dallied there for a while, almost wistfully, while the horse cropped the grass at the roadside. Then he moved on.

Dawn came with long streaks in the sky of indigo, grey and pink. Needing to remain unseen, the president spurred his horse into action and galloped between the sleeping villages along the highway out of the city.

In the half-light, he looked down and noticed that the horse's white mane had become dark in places. He put his hand out and touched one of the patches. It was damp. He put his finger to his mouth. Blood. The blood tasted like iron on his lips. He lifted his hand to feel the bandages on his neck. They were sodden. Despite the continuous loss of blood, there was no pain and he did not feel dizzy or faint.

He decided to stick to his original plan and galvanised the horse into a gallop once more. Soon there should be a turning that led to the Arawak village of Hicuri in the bush. It was not signposted but he thought he could recognise it. If he hid somewhere near there, he could seek help should it become necessary.

He turned down the small track that branched off the main highway. The horse picked its way through the puddles and lakes of the flooded savannah. Feeling too visible in the open country now that it was nearly daylight, the president left the wide trail with its sandy, rutted tracks and guided his horse across a patch of scrub towards the forest stretching away to his left.

Once under cover of the trees, he relaxed. There was a faint trail and he let the horse pick its own way through the stinging insects and slashing grasses. Not much light penetrated. The morning was humid. Sometimes he ducked to avoid tangled vines and lianas slapping him in the face. The horse stopped every now and then to chomp noisily on wild vegetation. After a while, they came to a place where the trees thinned out and the horse could wander more freely. Exhausted, the president fell into a profound sleep in the saddle.

The captain of Hicuri village was drunk as usual. Even so, he had managed to go into town and persuade the only man he knew who could mend televisions to accompany him back out to the village. The contraption he drove was a cross between Stephenson's Rocket engine, a tractor and a guillotine cart. The video technician, a scrawny East Indian with a straggly moustache, stood in the back. His leg was encased in plaster from ankle to thigh. Every time the vehicle jolted on the pitted red road that led to Hicuri, the man screeched with pain: 'Ooouw.'

The only other passenger returning to his village was a young Lokono Arawak called Calvin. Calvin had been working on the dredgers up on the Potaro River when he contracted malaria and had to be sent home. Now he shivered in the back, wracked with fits of icy fever and nausea.

It was Calvin who pointed out the trail of blood leading to the forest. The captain did not stop.

'You seein' ning-ning,' he shouted over his shoulder, thinking that Calvin was suffering the delusions that sometimes come with malaria. He himself, these days, often saw crystal balls and beetles.

In the village, the technician worked for an hour. When the villagers heard the generator start up, they began to gather under the open-sided palm-thatch shelter which housed the television and video machine. Old and young, everybody came walking across the grey sand, even Calvin, a towel wrapped round his waist and so weak that he had to lean against the shed post for support. They sat in rows on benches. Overhead, a parrot chattered non-stop in the scolding voice of an old woman.

The screen flickered and applause broke out. The technician inserted the video which he had brought with him to test the machine. He was proud of the video.

The whole country had been taken by surprise at the death of President Hercules the week before. He had gone into hospital for minor surgery and died under the anaesthetic. The Cuban doctors struggled to save his life, but to no avail. The technician had opportunistically jumped at the chance of videoing the funeral and hoped to sell the film. It was while he was running home to view it that he had broken his leg.

The state funeral of President Baldwin Hercules had taken place a week after his death and the day before the technician's visit to Hicuri.

The video opened with a blurry and confused shot of the funeral cortège. The gun carriage with the body, drawn by the president's own sweating white horse, was hurtling down Camp Street in the middle of a thunderstorm with people running alongside to keep up. Curious onlookers stood in the street, ducking the rain, some with newspapers covering their heads, others with umbrellas. Some just stood and stared as if something unpleasant was passing.

By all accounts, the body had suffered from the frequent power cuts while it was in the mortuary freezer. At one point, the mortuary assistants had taken it out and hung it upside-down in the local abattoir. Nor was the preservation of the corpse helped by the fact that one of the employees at the morgue had been found drunk on the embalming fluid. Haste was necessary if those attending the funeral were not to be overcome by the stench. The coffin was jolted so violently that both of the purple boots, emblem of the fallen warrior, had been tossed from the top into the street.

Then a sort of blizzard hit the screen. The villagers waited patiently while the technician explained that there was a gap in the video because he had had to make his way to the sepulchre for the rest of the ceremony.

The film came back on. Watching intently, the villagers saw the coffin being placed on the catafalque.

It was only when the solemn face of Edwin Jeffson appeared on the screen in close-up, giving the funeral oration with tears streaming down his face, that the Lokono Arawak villagers of Hicuri exploded spontaneously into howls of laughter. The more he wept, the more they laughed. They screeched and clutched each other, helpless with mirth, as each politician in turn was shown dabbing his or her eyes solemnly with a handkerchief and throwing flowers reverently on to the coffin. A wild hilarity swept through the whole village.

The sound of the laughter carried right out of Hicuri village, over the creek and into the far side of the forest where the white horse continued to put his head down and forage for grass. His ears twitched at the distant laughter. He ambled to the other side of the clearing, the revenant still asleep on his back. There, beneath the trees, the horse continued to graze patiently, until such time as his sleeping burden should wake again.

MRS DA SILVA'S
CARNIVAL

The shop isn't built that would sell a leotard Mrs da Silva's size.

No way can Mrs da Silva fit into a leotard – any leotard. The Mabaruma-warrior section of her carnival band is supposed to be wearing shiny copper leotards. Mrs da Silva is the mother of the band. She has been matriarch of Rebel War Band for longer than anyone can remember and has not missed one Notting Hill carnival since the whole caboodle began. The sight of Mrs da Silva's enormous behind, swinging rhythmically from side to side like a huge demolition ball capable of knocking down the houses on either side of the street, has inspired a multitude of revellers. After worried consultations between the band's designer and the various stitchers and sewers, it is agreed that Mrs da Silva must be outfitted with a voluminous dress of the same copper colour as the leotards. On the morning of the day, Mrs da Silva, out of breath but triumphant, climbs the stairs of the Hanley Road workshops to be garbed in a giant shimmering copper tent.

It is six months since Mrs da Silva suffered her setback. For twenty years, since her husband's departure, she had enjoyed an illicit affair with Pastor Fritz from the Evangelical Baptist church. At nights, her children would beg for peace as the sound of clacking dominoes and victorious shouts from their mother and Pastor Fritz kept them awake. Eventually, one winter evening long after the children had thankfully escaped into marriages of their own, the Pastor and Mrs da Silva sat on her green draylon settee, trays of food on their laps, concentrating on an episode of *Falconcrest* where the insane escapee from an asylum, dressed as a nun and having taken a small child hostage, is hiding in the gallery of a church with a shotgun, waiting to shoot the bride as she walks down the aisle towards her bridegroom.

Almost in unison they dip their spoons into dishes of creamy butter-bean soup crammed with yam, sweet potato, boiled plantain, onion and peppers. Just as the insane killer takes aim, Pastor Fritz, overcome by the delicious, steamy food and the comforting warmth of the occasion, turns to his long-time paramour and proposes marriage.

Dolly da Silva looks shy for a split second before accepting. A surge of affection, tinged with awe, overcomes her as she looks at him dabbing his lips with a paper kitchen towel, his balding head cocked on one side, waiting for an answer. After all, a pastor is a pastor. Not the least advantage of such a match would be the mortification of Mrs Bannerman when she heard the news. Mrs Bannerman had been conducting a mild flirtation with the Pastor for years and her behaviour had long been a source of irritation to Dolly da Silva.

'Of course I will marry you,' she said as the credits of *Falconcrest* rolled and he held out his plate for another helping of butter-bean soup.

The wedding was arranged for the first Saturday in March. Invitations went out to seventy-five guests. The holy-rolling, eye-swivelling, hand-clapping choir of Pastor Fritz's church solemnly agreed to sing at the ceremony. Her daughters arrived on the doorstep lugging giant aluminium pots for the goat curry. Her sons organised the transport and booked the hall.

The Friday before the wedding, Pastor Fritz, who now spent nearly all his time at Mrs da Silva's house helping with the arrangements, stuck his head round the door of the front room and told her that he was zooming out to get two more bags of rice.

But Pastor Fritz did not stop zooming. First of all he zoomed down to the Baptist church and removed all the church funds from the safe in the office. Then he zoomed along to Heathrow Airport and bought a ticket. Then he zoomed over to Madison, Ohio, from whence he never returned. Two months later, she received a postcard that said: 'Hi from Ohio.'

'All men are dogs,' said Mrs da Silva.

Mr Norman Foster, Mrs da Silva's Jamaican postman, had hesitated before delivering the postcard from Ohio. Unbeknownst to her, he had been keeping his own secret surveillance on her ever since his own wife died. This was because he knew she was a widow and, when he made his second delivery at midday, he often smelled mouth-watering aromas of fish stew with dumplings or curried chicken when he opened the letter box. He became wistful whenever he witnessed Pastor Fritz leaving the house in the mornings. He heard with concern and indignation about the wedding débâcle. His almost military formality forbade him from introducing himself but for some time he had hoped to find a way of becoming better acquainted with Mrs da Silva. With a frown he delivered the offensive postcard.

Mrs da Silva, meanwhile, experienced a bad feeling swilling around in the bottom of her stomach whenever she thought of Pastor Fritz. Now the house felt lonely with all her children gone and no more visits from the Reverend. It was only as carnival time drew near that she began to recover her spirits because carnival was the beginning and end of the year for her. She measured the passing of time by carnival. And with this carnival, the year that contained Pastor Fritz and the wedding fiasco would be swept aside and she could start afresh.

'Good mornin'.' Mrs da Silva is panting as she waddles through the door of Hanley Road workshops.

'Good morning, Mrs da Silva,' chorus the throng of amphibians and warriors in the women's changing rooms.

This year the theme is Rainforest and the band is divided into tree-frogs, Mabaruma warriors, Ciboney warriors, lizards and devils.

For months, the rooms of the Hanley Street community centre have witnessed girls and women hemming, cutting material, gluing, stitching, yawning, gaffin', limin', gossiping, quarrelling, painting and sticking costumes and accessories together.

Mrs da Silva finds her costume on a hanger behind the door. It has a warning note pinned to it: 'Mrs da Silva's costume. Don't piss with this. If you piss with this – you miss.'

As soon as Dolly da Silva is dressed in her bronze-coloured tabernacle, she sits on one of the rows of chairs near the door.

She is sixty-five years old and entitled to sit and fan herself while others rampage.

Pure mayhem is the order of the day. Sixty people dressing up and shouting for make-up sticks and ear-rings, head-bands, fans plaited from dried grasses, and everybody fixing up theyself and they friends, pushing each other out of the way of the mirror and grabbing the best armlets and anklets. Green lizards dart around looking for someone to help fasten their ridged crests. Mabaruma warriors are squawking as they delve into piles of accessories to find one of the tall head-dresses woven with fine cane and decked with feathers set aside for their section. Someone hands Mrs da Silva a grater from Woolworth's which she strings around her neck. In her hand she carries a cassava made of papier mâché and raffia. On her nose perches a pair of cheap, pink-rimmed spectacles through which she inspects the scene.

Her rival in life, Mrs Bannerman, a middle-weight sixty-two year old, puffs up the stairs and sits down next to her. Mrs Bannerman has scored over Mrs da Silva recently by becoming a widow herself and getting everybody's sympathy, a sympathy which Mrs da Silva resents more than ever because of Pastor Fritz's defection.

Mrs Bannerman has managed to shoehorn herself into a green tree-frog costume. Her eyes slide up and down Mrs da Silva's shapeless copper tent, taking in the sight with satisfaction. She preens herself a little and leans the giant leaf – which all tree-frogs must carry – against the wall:

'Hello, m'dear. How you do?' She lowers herself into the chair next to Mrs da Silva and continues without waiting for a reply. 'I did see Marjorie Taylor last night, you next-door neighbour. She very distress.' Mrs Bannerman is pleased both at Marjorie's distress and at being the first to tell Dolly da Silva about it.

Mrs da Silva grunts, annoyed with Marjorie that she should have got herself distressed without bothering to inform her, Mrs da Silva, first.

'What happen with her?' she asks grudgingly.

'Well,' said Mrs Bannerman conspiratorially. 'Yesterday Marjorie went shopping and bought some vegetables and so on and some liver. She came home and put the liver in the fridge. She went out back again to pick up one or two more things and when she came in back,' Mrs Bannerman lowered her voice in order not to alarm any of the younger women, 'the liver had got out of the fridge and was walking up de wall.'

Mrs da Silva adjusted her spectacles, leaned back and stared at Mrs Bannerman.

'What are you tellin' me? Yuh mad? Liver caan' walk.'

'I am tellin' you that the liver was walkin' up the wall. It was about so high off the ground.' Mrs Bannerman raised her hand above her head.

Mrs da Silva began to fidget with annoyance. She glared at Mrs Bannerman with scorn, then spoke to her as if she were a child.

'Mrs Bannerman. The liver ain' got no lungs. The liver caan' breathe, so how de liver can walk up de wall?'

'The liver did walk.' Mrs Bannerman bridled with resentment at Mrs da Silva's scepticism.

'The liver don' have legs,' Mrs da Silva continued with infuriating logic, 'and so the liver caan' walk.'

'The liver mussa did crawl.'

'And how it did open the fridge door?'

'I'll tell you,' said Mrs Bannerman, bristling, the colour rising in the face. 'The liver come from a cow. The cow had cancer and cancer is a livin' thing. THAT'S how the liver could walk up de wall,' she announces, triumphantly.

Silenced by this coup de science, Mrs da Silva snaps her mouth shut like a turtle and clenches her fists secretly under her costume. By god's grace, she is saved from further humiliation at the hands of Mrs Bannerman by the explosive arrival of the band's designer, Lulu Banks.

Lulu, double-chinned, hair piled high, bursts in, late and hysterical, having frightened all the other drivers on the Hornsey Road by leaning out of her car window in full lizard gear, to offer them colourful abuse at their slow progress. She wrinkles her nose at the smell of greasepaint, glue, old gauze, paint and sweat before wading directly into the maelstrom.

She bangs both hands on the table and shouts, 'All tree-frogs please make sure you are carrying a giant leaf. Mrs da Silva, you need a head-dress. The head-dresses are in a pile by the radiator.'

Grateful for the excuse to move out of Mrs Bannerman's superiority zone, Dolly da Silva shuffles over and fishes out a head-dress from the tangle of grabbing arms.

'Where's my costume?' A hand flicks down the rail where each person's outfit hangs labelled, finds the leotard and snatches it up. Some of the band are Amerindian warriors. Some are tree-frogs and green lizards. The men are divided into warriors with a small section of tree-frogs and an even smaller section of traditional devils with tails and three-pronged forks.

Amidst the bustle of Mabaruma tribeswomen fixing their faces with lipstick and sticky sequins and sparkle dust, people are beginning to steal each other's accessories. Filching on a mammoth scale takes place – head-bands, neck ornaments, spray paint. A tall female warrior with skinny breasts is wrestling with a child for a pole with a fan on it.

'Just let me hold it for a minute. I'll give it back to you, I promise.' The child relinquishes the pole and the girl scoots down the stairs with it and settles in one of the vans waiting outside to carry the band.

Downstairs, the yard is a turmoil of tree-frogs, lizards and warriors trying to sort out the big blue canoe on wheels that is supposed to be the centrepiece. A brown dummy stretches luxuriously in the boat. Mrs da Silva's eldest son Cuthbert, an exemplary devil with red horns, is brandishing his trident trying to direct the operation. He stops for a moment and moves away from the noise, cupping a hand over one ear while he makes a call on the mobile phone to his wife who is in the first stages of labour at St Mary's Hospital.

'Everything all right, Jean?' he shouts over the pandemonium in the background. 'You've got this number. Ring me when it gets close and I'll be right there. The route is near the hospital so I can be there in a tick. Bye, sweetheart.' He dashes to save the dummy from being tipped out of the canoe.

Upstairs, Mrs da Silva is fighting gamely with a wig of coarse black raffia hair that is supposed to go under her head-dress.

Scoobie, Mrs da Silva's other son, a council education officer disguised as a tree-frog, is standing next to the truck listening to his hand-held radio. This year the police have been issuing warnings about violence. They are expecting violence. They are anticipating hand-bag grabbers. They are prophesying lost children. They are foreseeing the picking of a million pockets. They are predicting muggers. They are extinguishing joy wherever possible. They are announcing doom over the airwaves. Scoobie pulls a dismal face. Then he hears another item of news on the local radio station. Scoobie lets out a cheer. Rebel War Band's greatest local rival, Tigermonger Band, is stuck in the warehouse because their giant butterfly wings are too huge to pass through the doors. Right there on the pavement, Scoobie performs a natty, triumphal dance that involves much hip and groin movement.

Lulu, already hoarse, is now yelling in the street, 'Tree-frogs and lizards. Will you please line up for your photographs.'

Everybody mills around.

She makes last-minute adjustments to people's costumes, tying a headscarf here, instructing someone else to wear bangles, adjusting wigs, reminding warriors to carry their bows and arrows. Gradually, under the grey sky, tree-frogs, lizards, Mabaruma warriors and devils have their photographs taken outside the dismal, pre-cast concrete community centre and settle down in the three mini-buses waiting to leave. The moving pyramid which is Mrs da Silva makes a dignified descent down the iron staircase to the yard. Avoiding the mini-bus containing Mrs Bannerman she clambers inside another one, taking up two seats amidst a forest of spears, one of which occasionally jooks her in the neck.

Lulu Banks is raging on the pavement. All the mini-bus seats are taken. There is no room for her. No one will budge to give up their seat. Tears of frustration spring into her eyes. Everyone looks somewhere else, gazing out of the window, staring down at their laps as she stomps up and down the street.

'I am never doing the designs again. This is the last straw.

Is pure selfishness. I never playin' maas again.' Finally, she yells in fury, 'You all are behavin' like white people.'

Some music starts up from the truck. The street is momentarily filled with pan music jangling in the background as the familiar voice on tape blams out:

Rant, rant, rant, rant,
Rant and rave,
Ho-old something
And misbehave.

Lulu Banks, in full lizard gear, is magically transformed, sweetened in an instant by the music. She stops yelling and starts to wind her waist. Soon her hips are moving suggestively, her behind wagging its provocative little lizard tail, her arms raised in the air. The lofty grey council blocks on either side of the street look down on her. Smiling and with an expression of sexual bliss on her face, she lays down a serious pattern of steps on the pavement. Somebody laughs and claps. There is a round of applause and a cheer and whooping. People shift up and she climbs on board, beaming.

Two hours late, the band sets off. The truck with the towering sound system and the dummy in the canoe follows on behind.

On arrival at the appointed spot, having successfully negotiated the van under the bridge by the flyover, Cuthbert and Scoobie wave their passes and argue bitterly with police, stewards and organisers about their route and the starting point. Eventually, Rebel War Band draws up in a side road off Ladbroke Grove.

Mrs da Silva tries to uncork herself from the mini-bus doors. She steps into a nearly empty street and looks round in anger.

She adjusts her spectacles and announces, 'The police are wicked. Look how they frighten people away.'

Last year, she had descended into the street dressed as Nefertiti to be greeted by cheers from stall-holders and breakdancers, smells of sizzling jerk pork and general street uproar. Disgruntled, she goes to the truck and checks that the seventy-eight portions of escoveitch fish, one hundred and thirty portions of fried chicken, coleslaw, and bread rolls, are safely in the back alongside the two hundred cartons of tropical fruit juice.

She squints up at the sky. The weather is warm and dull. It might even rain. In a pouch hanging round her neck is a medicine bottle filled with Old Oak rum. She screws off the top and takes a small sip.

The music strikes up from the truck and the sixty-odd masqueraders of Rebel War Band take up position in a disorderly manner in front of the sound truck. The band moves off. Mrs da Silva has placed herself at the front with the devil men who are in harness attached to the dummy trundling along in his canoe. Around her are the Mabaruma warriors with their nose-rings, blow-pipes and bows and arrows. Behind all these are the Ciboney tribe dressed in dazzling yellow leotards with fans attached to their backs. Then come the black tree-frogs, each one partnered by a green tree-frog, followed by the lime-green lizards.

Crowds now line the pavement on either side and Mrs da Silva begins to concentrate on allowing the tingalang pangalang of the music to enter her bones. She shakes her body, shimmying to and fro, and stamps her feet down in the hip-swinging carnival shuffle. Mrs da Silva shimmying is like an earthquake in motion. She takes another tipple of rum. Quite soon she begins to feel better. Before long her head-dress has turned back to front and her spectacles are at an odd angle, but the puddle of gloom that has been swilling at the bottom of her stomach for several months begins to evaporate.

She shimmies backwards and deliberately steps hard on Mrs Bannerman's foot.

'Sorry, daalin'.' Smiling sweetly over her shoulder, she shuffles forward again, singing along whole-heartedly as the volume of sound on the truck is turned up:

> Oh I want to get a divorce
> Because my wife she looks like a horse . . .

Suddenly, the truck lurches to a halt and the music skids down an octave to a stop. The members of Rebel War Band gradually cease dancing and look around to see what's happening. The band behind pulls slowly out and to Mrs da Silva's disgust, Rebel War is overtaken by a collection of giant sea-shells and shrimps who slowly waver alongside with tentacles and antennae dipping and bobbing.

'Every year it's the same. Every year it's the same thing,' shrieks Mrs da Silva. She elbows out of the way a skeleton with a policeman's helmet pushing a cart who just happens to be passing and makes her way back through the revellers towards the sound truck.

'Keep calm, Mummy. We just got to put more juice in the generator,' Cuthbert explains apologetically, his painted devil's face sweating and screwed up with strain. The stewards lower the rope that keeps the band intact and contained. Disgruntled frogs and lizards, who were just getting into the swing, sit on the kerbside. Mrs da Silva stands guard impatiently over the store of food stashed in the back of the vehicle.

Finally, they get going again. The sun puts in an appearance. Grey skies lighten into blue.

With judicious manoeuvring, they slot in again between the Perpetual Beauty Band of shrimps and sea-shells and Jet Jewels, a band that has brought the Haitian spirit of Baron Samedi to the streets of England. Pinned to their shoulders, the men bear giant effigies, of Baron Samedi in top hat, gloves and dark glasses. The women wear the downy feathers of white sensa fowl and a section of great white butterflies prances delicately along covered with powdery snow. At their side a fifteen-foot-tall stilt-man in glittering white rags and a white mask makes threatening, darting movements towards them all with his white-gloved hands.

In Rebel War Band, Mystery Mandy, whose second name no one knows and who materialises only once a year at carnival, is drunk again and lying on her back in the road, lifting her pelvis up and down. One of the other girls straddles her and their bodies gyrate together, then everyone piles on top, until she disappears in a mass of winding hips and the crowd pushes in close to witness this outrageous act of simulated group sex on the streets of Notting Hill until all the revellers spring apart and dance off down the road, grinning and laughing.

Mrs da Silva beams around at everybody. She has been winding what little waist she has all morning, stopping to walk when she becomes too short of breath. It is turning out to be a good carnival after all. The only mishap has been when her young niece Dawn collapsed in agony and was last seen being handed over the heads of the crowd by the St John Ambulance Brigade, like a canoe bobbing on water. People argue over whether it's peritonitis or a perforated ulcer but Mrs da Silva guesses that it's just period pains. She has some St John's bush at home which she will take round if the pains don't cease by the next day.

They stop for lunch, pulling into a pre-arranged side street of tall and seedy white-painted houses with flaking porticoes. Eager hands reach for portions of fish and chicken and cartons of drink. Mrs da Silva stands beside the truck supervising the distribution of the food which, like the miracle of the loaves and the fishes, multiplies itself to feed everybody.

On the road again, hot and breathing hard, Mrs da Silva pounds and shakes through the afternoon, sweat gleaming on her forehead in the sun. For the first time since his departure, Mrs da Silva has forgotten about Pastor Fritz. She feels as if some old, unused engine has kicked into action again. And it is still in working order. She feels good. Once a year, the centre of the street is her rightful place. She looks up at the houses on either side and at the onlookers who are crammed in the windows, balancing on parapets, putting their feet up on the ledges and balconies as they tilt bottles of beer towards their mouths. Mrs da Silva waves joyously although her feet are beginning to ache.

Cuthbert da Silva is driving the truck at snail's pace in order not to trap members of the band under its wheels. He watches his mother move backwards and forwards. The windscreen is covered with bits of confetti and gold dust. He is just peering ahead when his mobile phone rings. He puts it to his ear and can't hear a thing above the song which is belting out from the back:

Kingston hot hot hot,
Kingston hot hot hot.

'What? I caan' hear.' He bangs the machine on his lap, controlling the vehicle with his left hand.

He can't hear a word but he knows what it is and slams on the brakes.

'Scoobie. Take over this vehicle. I gotta find the hospital.'

Scoobie slides into the driver's seat and watches Cuthbert's three-pronged trident work its way through the crowd.

Twenty minutes later a muscular devil with stubby horns, fork, a black-and-red torso and painted legs stuck with tufts of goat hair is queuing up at the reception desk of St Mary's Hospital, asking where the labour ward is.

Two hours later, a tiny infant, fifteen minutes old, opens his eyes briefly in the delivery room, looks up from his father's arms and knows that life is going to be a nightmare.

Back on the carnival route, the band has found its second wind and dances relentlessly on. Lulu Banks takes up position on the truck with a megaphone.

'Rebel War Band. Get into your sections, please. We are approaching the judging point. Get into your sections, PLEASE,' she screams. 'Mabaruma men and devils first – pushing the dummy. Then Ciboney and Mabaruma women. Then tree-frogs. Lizards at the back.'

Mrs da Silva is taken by surprise at the announcement.

She has somehow worked her way to the back and is firmly wedged among the green lizards. She hacks her way out with a cassava. She gets back in front. Three shrimps with huge antennae have fallen back from the float in front and are wandering amongst the Mabaruma warriors.

'GET OUT, SHRIMPS. WILL ALL SHRIMPS PLEASE FUCK OFF? YOU'RE SPOILING OUR CHANCES.'

Lulu's eyes are shining with tears of hysteria. Mrs da Silva attacks the offending crustaceans with her grater and sees them off. The band proceeds to the judging point. Mrs da Silva is now leading the band, head thrown back, arms stretched out in front of her as if she has just triumphantly levered herself off a crucifix. She doesn't see the uniformed policeman, who only just avoids being absorbed into the oscillating copper mushroom that is Mrs da Silva. The jangling music pumps out and she sings along:

> Shut you mouth, go away,
> Mamma look a booboo deh.
> That's you mamma there. Oh no,
> My mamma can't be ugly so.

For the five minutes it takes to pass the judging point, the sections are in their correct order and everybody winds and smiles and looks cute and bows to the judges on their rostrum but Lulu Banks is sobbing because the dummy, which had all along looked too serious for the occasion, has chosen that moment of all moments to make a suicide bid and throw itself from the canoe.

'GET THE DUMMY BACK IN THE BOAT.' Lulu throws down the megaphone and collapses weeping and hyperventilating in the back of the truck next to the unconscious Mandy.

'You all can do it yourselves next year.' A trail of tears glistens down her cheeks. Someone hands her an aluminium bottle of rum and fruit juice.

Mrs da Silva's eyes are almost closed in ecstasy.

'Let the police hit themselves up they own backside,' she chortles defiantly as the band plays. 'This is Madness.'

Past the judging point, the hill slopes upward and Mrs da Silva, puffing heavily, slows down to a walk.

Striding alongside Rebel War Band, apologising as he steps on the toes of the crowd, is Mr Norman Foster, Mrs da Silva's neighbourhood postman. Dressed as a headmistress, he is wearing pink lipstick, a hairnet and respectable tweeds. He puts on a spurt in order to catch up with her.

Norman Foster is a Jamaican of the patriarchal variety, with a sprig of a moustache and stiff bearing. He has always considered carnival to be foolishness, a batty-man business instigated by crazy Trinidadians, probably because of the inferior quality of their rum. However, he knew that Mrs da Silva played maas religiously each year and he sensed that this might be his only chance to woo her. The problem was that he did not belong to a band and all through the summer, pride and raised hackles at the thought prevented him from asking how he might join the Rebel War Band.

All heroes must go through an ordeal to win their lady. Norman Foster had left it too late to join Mrs da Silva's band. His retirement had gone through the week before. His loneliness bore down on him as he realised that he would no longer pass Dolly da Silva's front door twice a day on his postman's round and he appreciated for the first time how much of his emotional life revolved round the possibility of seeing her.

And so, on the morning of carnival, with some anguish, he went up to his bedroom and took his wife's clothes out of the cupboard where they had remained since her death four years earlier. He laid them on the bed, went down on his knees beside the bed and spoke.

'Hilda. I want fi you to help me one more time. I know you wouldn't want me to be lonely. I tink I have a chance with Mrs da Silva. I don' want fi you to be jealous. I always have the greatest respeck for you. But I tired to keep struggling on my own here. I hope you could hunderstand.'

It seemed to him that the clothes said yes.

Norman Foster proceeded to dress up in his wife's large tweed skirt, a pale-pink sweater and the jacket which matched the skirt. He put on a lipstick he had discovered in one of her old handbags and donned a hairnet. Then, in an act of hitherto unhinted-at courage, Norman Foster, senior postal officer with the Royal Mail, strode down the path to his front gate and stepped out into Victoria Road, Hornsey. Looking neither to right nor left and with his eyes fixed far ahead of him, he marched down the road and caught a bus to Westbourne Park Road, ignoring the stifled giggles of the other passengers. He then spent most of the day pushing through crowds, booming sound systems and patty stalls, scurrying up and down, having his feet trodden on, anxiously scanning the floats and trucks. His bottom had been pinched twice before he caught sight of Mrs da Silva.

'Mrs da Silva.'

Without breaking her step, she turns to see who is calling her.

'Mrs da Silva.' She looks at him, puzzled, panting and still shuffling gaily forwards.

'It's me, your postman.'

She peers at the anxious, tweed-suited, hair-netted figure running along beside the band and her face cracks open ito a big smile.

'Mr Postman. You look like you could do with some refreshment.' She takes the flask of rum from round her neck and hands it to him. Gratefully, he takes a swig.

'Mrs da Silva.' Made dizzy by the joyous cacophony of the music and the gaily wobbling figure in front of him, he seizes his chance.

'Mrs da Silva, you lookin' splendacious. I live on my own and I am quite lonely. I would like to call on you one day. I am retired from the Post Office now and I don' have too much to do.'

'Come in the evening on Thursday,' Mrs da Silva shouts over the noise. She always sits with her feet in a bucket of hot water for two days after Bank Holiday Monday's carnival.

Then: 'Stewards, please to lift up the rope and let in the postman.'

Norman Foster ducked under the rope and for the next half an hour Rebel War Band is led by a smiling Mrs da Silva accompanied by a rather prim-stepping, school-mistressy creature with a moustache who seems quite overcome by the occasion.

It is dusk when Rebel War Band comes to the finishing point under the concrete and steel arches of the Westway. Amid a dereliction of giant golden insects and collapsed angels, Mr Foster says goodbye to Mrs da Silva and goes home, his heart singing.

On Thursday evening, Mrs da Silva answers a rap on the door. The butter-bean soup is bubbling gently and enticingly on the stove.

She looks through the peep-hole and then shouts through the door, 'Are you pretty?'

'I believe so,' smiles Mr Foster, standing in the drizzle.

'Are you the same pretty person I dance with on Monday?'

'The very same,' says Mr Foster coyly. And Mrs da Silva opens the door, a plate of soup in her hand, to welcome him in.

THE *DUENDE*

On the morning of the fiftieth anniversary of her husband's death, Doña Rosita awoke and decided to do things differently.

She left her old, iron-frame bed in the corner of the room and went over to the jug and bowl of water on the table beneath the window. After she had washed, she splashed herself over with the water as if blessing herself from a font. Truly refreshed, wiping herself with a towel, she crossed the room still wearing her nightdress. The bed creaked as she sat down heavily on the edge of it. She looked at her feet on the wooden floor. A slip of sunlight lay slantwise across them.

Outside, the neighbourhood dogs set up their usual harsh barking as her son-in-law herded the sheep along the dusty yellow road past the rusty corrugated iron of the cowshed and towards the fields. Prickly pear climbed higgledy-piggledy along the stone wall where the flock passed. A yellow road and a yellow wind, thought Doña Rosita. Later in the morning, under the blazing sun, the road would turn white.

For several minutes, Doña Rosita examined the bare feet placed firmly apart on the worn wood of the floor. Despite her eighty-two years, her feet remained as flexible as those of a young woman. Their appearance was gnarled and twisted like an olive tree. But, she thought, as she wriggled her toes, even the most ancient olive tree still has sap running. That's what gives the touch of greenness to the grey. Her feet felt lively. She studied them and flexed the right one up and down on the ball of her foot. Yes. For some reason, on this particular morning, her feet felt strong and independent as if they had a will of their own.

'Today, I shall go wherever you carry me,' she addressed her feet, and then cackled, 'as if I could go anywhere else, come to think of it.'

There were only three articles of furniture in the room: the high bed with one blanket, whose sheets barely needed straightening because she moved so little in her sleep; the table which served as a washstand and an old dark wooden wardrobe by the door. The lack of other furniture gave these three items a sombre weight, an importance of which Doña Rosita was unaware as she moved slowly from one to the other, carrying out the various functions with which she prepared for the day.

Four black dresses hung in the wardrobe. She lifted one from the rail and frowned at it. She had first worn black as a thirty-two-year-old woman after her husband's sudden death. Then other people had died, sporadically, but in an endless succession – friends, relatives, neighbours – and she never again found the opportunity to be dressed in colour. Since that time she had been obliged to wear nothing but black. All the dresses were the same length, down to her knees. All had the same V-shaped neck and sleeves that came halfway to her elbows. Because of many years' wear, they all carried the sharp tang of sweat beneath the arms, despite careful laundering. When Christmas came or a saint's day, she put a comb in her hair which had grown silver in the time since that first death and fastened three handsome strands of jet beads around her neck. On special occasions, she would also take out her black-lace fan – the one with the ivory inlay – from the top of the wardrobe.

Whenever one of the dresses wore out, she took the bus and made a pilgrimage to Jerez de la Frontera. First she would visit her friend Alba who worked in the dark interior of her husband's draper's shop.

Alba's complexion intrigued Doña Rosita because it was so unlike her own. While they sipped milky coffee from glasses in silvered containers and nibbled biscuits, the two women discussed the affairs of their households, and Rosita always marvelled afresh at that creamy white skin, soft like dough, and at the pale brown of her friend's eyes. When they were younger, Alba's brown hair reached halfway down her back and she would perch on a bolt of cloth like a mermaid at the bottom of the ocean. Then, throughout the years of their maturity, childless Alba, married to a gnome of a man who played trumpet in the local band, served coffee from her chair, staying just out of reach of the sunlight that fell through the door from the street outside. In later times, a younger woman served in the shop but Alba remained seated in the shadows. Through sitting for so many years in the dark among the piled rolls and bolts of cloth, Alba had managed always to avoid the midday sun and it seemed that the sole purpose of her life had been to win a victory over this solar enemy, who would now never find an opportunity to affect the pallor of her skin – although liver-spots had done a certain amount of work on her face as she grew older.

When the coffee, and biscuits with delicate rice paper at the base were finished, Rosita would select a length of black cloth, pay for it, thank Alba kindly for the refreshment and walk two doors up to the dressmaker.

Rosita did not like the dressmaker so much. The bespectacled woman always seemed to be in a hurry, stubbing out a cigarette as she darted here and there, searching for pins and tape-measures. Her children were allowed to be noisy. The woman let the radio blare while she measured Rosita. She and her husband frequented the modern dance-halls.

Even as a young woman, Rosita belonged to the old school.

In her youth and before her marriage, Rosita's heart had been taken up for a while with the gypsy *siguiriya* songs she heard at the Taberna Verde in Jerez de la Frontera. People came there to sing and to dance flamenco in the cabaret. Forbidden to visit such places by her father, she sneaked out a few times on the pretext of ministering to a sick friend. Then she and Alba would slip into the long, dark room, which reeked of burning lamp-oil fumes. In the *taberna*, packed with bodies, they would listen to musicians who could make them shudder and set their new breasts tingling with the death rattle of their guitars and the sobbing in their voices.

One regular performer of the *siguiriya* was a young gypsy man with a hookah tattooed on his neck. The anguish in his voice and the unexpectedly breathtaking silences of the deep song made Rosita's palms turn sweaty and her hair stand on end. People said that he was in the Foreign Legion, stationed at Aubagne in the South of France, but that every year at this time, when the gypsies passed through, he discarded his uniform, absented himself and came with them to sing.

Those few clandestine visits to the Taberna Verde took place in her early adolescence before her husband had even begun to think of courting her. In those days she was driven by a passionate desire to dance flamenco. Whenever she was at home on her own, the sturdy, serious fourteen year old practised those heel-clicking steps, holding her arms aloft in the shape of a bull's horns and swivelling her hips, following their lead with her eyes. The cool, gloomy entrance to their yellowing limestone house was laid with darkly patterned tiles that enabled her to hear the drumming rhythms of her heels clearly, and she practised until she was exhausted under the sad eyes of the Virgin Mary whose picture hung on the wall.

But, although she longed to do so, she never dared to get up on the stage and perform in the *taberna* as did some of the other girls. And gradually, the phase passed and she could hardly remember the shivers and fast pulse-rate of her early puberty. She stayed at home, working with her mother who taught her to make lace, and, according to what the seasons required, she helped the rest of the family on the land when it was time to pick tomatoes or olives.

Rosita, at the age of nineteen and not remarkably pretty – her lower jaw stuck out too squarely – had married the best-looking man in the village. His hair was black as a crow's feathers and he had wide-set eyes, greeny-blue as if the Mediterranean sea had been poured into them. Rosita concluded later, when life in the vast acreage of time lived without him had given her more experience, that, fortunately for her, he had never realised how good-looking he was. When she was much older still, she realised that there is something a little lacking in a man who does not appreciate his own good looks and who has no idea how to take advantage of such a god-given asset.

'Perhaps my Manuel was even a little stupid,' she sighed as the thought occurred to her.

Years later, after her husband's death at an early age, she suffered from guilt because when her neighbour had come banging on the door that hot afternoon shouting that he had been found dying in the street, the news pierced her in exactly the same way as the *siguiriya* songs had done and she wondered if the one had been a portent of the other. She felt that the songs were connected to his death and that he died because she had heard it and not understood that it was a warning for the future.

The story of her husband's death was both tragic and simple. Each morning of their married life, she packed up olives, bread and cheese, some tomatoes and lemonade for his lunch. He worked at the limestone quarry and preferred to eat there in the dazzling white crater, rather than face a long walk home in the midday sun. The couple had waited nearly ten years until their long hoped-for first child arrived. She was two years old at this time. They both adored her. Rosita stayed at home to watch over her precious toddler.

Manuel carried a bone-handled, fold-up knife in the pocket of his overalls, as did all the men. The knife was used to cut bread or sever a rope that had become entangled round a limestone block, or cut a prickly pear off the branch to eat. It had a thousand and one uses.

Coming home one May afternoon, with the white quarry dust stinging his eyes and covering his workman's coarse dungarees, Rosita's husband was thirsty. He climbed on some loose boulders by the stone wall to cut himself a prickly pear. He slipped, doubled up, and the knife seized the unexpected opportunity to enter under his ribs and kill him. By the time Rosita came flying down the hill, he was already dead with a frilly carnation of blood blooming halfway down his white shirt where the knife had entered.

The whole village watched as the men shouldered the coffin, silhouetted against the empty sky, and trudged, in their best suits, over the arid, sun-baked fields, then down the slope alongside the dried river bed towards the churchyard, Rosita and her small daughter following behind.

As Doña Rosita studied the black dress in her hand, she wished she had something more colourful to wear that would suit her mood that morning. But she owned no other dresses. She put on the black dress that smelled least stale. Then she caught sight of a bunch of withered myrtle that she had nailed up by the window years before. She unhooked it and threw the dried twigs and leaves out of the window on to the street.

Downstairs, she poked her finger through the bars of the canary's cage to say good morning to the dingy bird and sat down to eat the breakfast her daughter had prepared for her.

Every day, in that village four miles from Jerez de la Frontera, people were accustomed to seeing Doña Rosita. When she had breakfasted on olive bread, goat cheese and a small cup of black coffee, she would collect her lace-making equipment and place her low stool just outside the front door in the sunshine. There she squatted, the bobbins clicking gaily as her fingers automatically drew the threads, deftly tossing the bobbins, one across the other, around the spindle. Doña Rosita had for years fabricated slow-moving glaciers of lace: the edging of pillow-slips, tablecloths, the lace borders of confirmation dresses and mantillas, the snowy hems of petticoats, ruches and lace collars for blouses. She was a fixture in the village. Other women often joined her to make lace and to chat, bringing their own spindles and bobbins. She was always there unless illness or a rare thunderstorm, a wedding or a funeral prevented it. Just before midday she would go into the cool of the house and emerge again at about half-past three for another hour or so.

On this morning, however, overtaken by uncontrollable restlessness, Doña Rosita's feet decided to take her for a walk. Her daughter had already left to work in the fields. She locked the house and set off up the sandy road, past the spiteful briars that clung to the dry-stone wall, ignoring the stray, scrawny yellow dog that swayed in the middle of the street like a high-noon cowboy.

At the top of the hill she stopped to look out over the bare, parched scene, the stone-walled fields white and colourless as a moonscape and the dark patch of the Peña family's lemon grove in the valley. A sickeningly warm wind blew. She continued until she came to the quarry which opened suddenly to the right of the path. It was silent. No one was working there. She wondered about her husband's last day at work and imagined him climbing up to this very spot to take his path home. Since that day, her own life seemed to have remained motionless. She stared down into the quarry. It looked much the same as when she was a young girl, a little bigger perhaps. A small brown bird sang fearlessly on a dusty shrub next to her. She looked north past the quarry.

The landscape looked exactly as it had done all her life. In the morning haze, the white square buildings of the next village two miles away remained unchanged. Nothing had altered. Everything seemed to have stayed the same under the weight of eternity.

Doña Rosita suddenly had an overwhelming desire for change before it was too late.

Slowly, she walked on down the other side of the hill towards the cemetery. The visit to the quarry made her husband's death seem to have happened only yesterday. The fresh ache somehow served to make her feel more alive.

At the cemetery, under a hazy sky, she sat down by the burning stone of her husband's grave and patted the dry earth.

'Manuel. I feel in need of a change. I hope you don't mind. It's just that I feel time has been standing still and I would like to start it moving before I come and join you.'

A short walk later she reached the next village and stood by the yellow wall of a house under the metal Coca-Cola sign that hung squeaking in the breeze. The wind fluttered her black dress against her bow legs. Now the road was white. In the distance, the noon bus came into sight, caked with dust from its twice-daily journey into town and back. It wound along the road and dipped out of sight. Ten minutes later, it stopped and Doña Rosita clambered on and bought a ticket to Jerez de la Frontera.

'Where are you off to?' asked a woman passenger, screwing up her face in undisguised curiosity at the unusual sight of Doña Rosita clambering on to the bus.

'I'm going to town,' she replied. 'I have business there.

I'm going to kick up my heels,' she joked. In fact, she had no idea what she was going to do.

As the bus manoeuvred down the steep part of the road past her own house, Doña Rosita looked at the spot where she normally sat as if she half expected to see herself there.

She got off the bus by the clothes market near the main square. It was a relaxed and innocent sort of market. The stall-holders seemed to be there as a form of courtesy rather than through an urgent desire to sell. They sat by their mounds of T-shirts and kiddies' short pants, gents' trousers and cheap dresses, some of which had been pegged out on lines for display, and watched, smiling, as passers-by lifted up the goods and inspected them.

Doña Rosita walked past the market, downhill towards the only place with which she was really familiar – the draper's shop.

Inside was so dark after the glaring sun, it was like going underwater. She could barely see whether her friend Alba was still there or not. Then she saw the tiny pale face in the dark. The shop assistant came out from the back and greeted Doña Rosita.

'Doña Alba doesn't speak to us any more, but you can sit with her as long as you want. I will fetch you both a lemon tea and a sandwich. We don't have any coffee at the moment.' She set about shutting up the shop for the afternoon siesta.

Doña Rosita pulled up a cane chair and sat opposite her friend who did not appear to recognise her.

'Good afternoon, Alba. It's good to see you after all this time.'

Her friend's white hands fumbled with the skirt of her

dress. Rosita leaned forward to look more closely at her. Her face was still almost youthfully plump but there was only vacancy behind the faded brown eyes set in their two dark, olive-coloured sockets.

Alba's mind has gone fishing, thought Rosita.

Then she did something she had always wanted to do. She gently pinched Alba's face to see if the skin felt as soft and doughy as it looked. It did. She ran a finger along the leathery hide of her own face and marvelled at the difference.

All afternoon, Rosita sat and talked to her friend who made no acknowledgement of her presence, but occasionally pulled the flesh of her face back with her hands into a sort of grimace, as if to say she had somehow wasted the whole of her life in the shadows, trying to keep pale. Rosita gave her all the latest news, quite matter-of-factly, about her own daughter and son-in-law, the condition of the sheep, the likelihood of a big tomato harvest this year, the Bishop's forthcoming tour of the neighbourhood. When Doña Alba knocked her lemon tea to the ground, Rosita rescued the glass and wiped Alba's skirt down.

After a while, Rosita too lapsed into silence and both women fell into a quiet doze in the dark. She was woken by the assistant opening up the shop again which she always did between the hours of four and six o'clock.

'I will stay with Alba until you close,' said Rosita, 'and before I leave I should like to buy some cloth.'

At a quarter to six, the assistant reached down the two bolts of black cloth from the second shelf behind the counter.

'No,' said Doña Rosita, using the arms of the chair to lever herself up, as she had become a little stiff. 'I want to see what colours you have.'

The assistant, excited by this change in routine, enthusiastically pulled down some brightly coloured bolts of scarlet and blue cloth.

'I don't want to go mad,' said Doña Rosita firmly. 'Get me down the green one there and the maroon.'

The green was dark like the leaves of an orange tree.

'That one,' she said.

With the parcel under her arm and having said goodbye to her absent friend, Rosita stepped out into the pleasant evening just as it was becoming dusk.

There was one other thing she wanted to do.

The road down to where the Taberna Verde had once been was steep with large, flat cobbles still warm from the day's sun. Doña Rosita made her way to the bottom of the town, past the rows of smaller, more expensive shops, past the police station and the post office to where the town levelled out near the bus terminal.

The Taberna Verde was still there. It had a new glass front and the sign-painter had done a good job of painting a guitar and a gaily fluttering ribbon on either side of the name. The pavement was too narrow for there to be any tables and chairs outside, but a hand-written placard announced the flamenco competition that was already in progress. Reflection from the glass stopped Doña Rosita from seeing inside properly. But she could hear the muffled strumming of a guitar and the familiar, stomping shuffle of feet on boards that made her feel as excited as she had been when she was fourteen.

She pushed open the door and went in.

Inside, everything had changed. There were electric lights and round metal tables with chairs instead of the long, dark benches and tables that she had known as a girl.

Tall mirrors hung along the walls between lurid, life-size paintings of famous bull-fighters. But the wooden stage was the same, ancient and even more scuffed than she remembered. Competitors and performers sat at the front tables. The singers wore jeans and shirts, the dancers wore traditional flamenco dress. The judges sat a little further back at one table.

Doña Rosita placed her package on the floor and sat down at one of the back tables. The place was half full. A waiter in black with a white apron swivelled around, flicked her table with a napkin and asked for her order.

She ordered a Manzanilla sherry. On stage, a lithe fair-haired girl of about fourteen was performing a traditional flamenco solo. Her twists and turns were full of a vigour and energy that was attractive because of her exuberance, but wasted somehow because she did not understand how to contain the feeling so that it burned slowly for everyone to enjoy. She won a good round of applause all the same.

I could show you a thing or two, thought Doña Rosita, who kept one foot touching her package in case anyone tried to pinch it. She sipped the sherry and felt it begin to work through her old body. An animated couple, a plump girl and a young man with oiled, crinkly, reddish hair and smudged freckles, made their way over to Doña Rosita and asked if they could sit at her table. She took her bag off the chair to make room for them. The *taberna* was starting to fill up.

Rosita leaned sideways so that she could observe the performers. She caught herself looking for the familiar figure of the man with the hookah tattoed on his neck. But he was not there. And she realised that by now he would be in his eighties too. Probably dead, she thought.

The sherry made her head feel light. Cigarette smoke hung in front of the dark paintings on the walls. She should have brought her fan. The *taberna* was beginning to bustle. She shifted in her seat to stop getting stiff. After an hour or so, the first singer of the *siguiriya* came on to the stage. Rosita craned to get a good view of the skinny young man with black hair, his sharp face concave like a crescent moon.

He was impressive. Rosita broke out into a sweat of pleasure. The audience whistled appreciation as the tension mounted during the song. The *taberna* was now so crowded she could barely see the stage. The waiter pushed his way through and put more Manzanilla sherry on their table. The young couple were on their feet applauding. The singer bowed and stepped to one side.

Another *siguiriya* singer took his place. The audience erupted with delight as his guitar wept and wailed like a trapped demon. The song sounded to Rosita like a battle against death. She held her breath, willing life to continue after the silences in the song, thinking that she would burst with the suspense of those unexpected silences. He started a new song:

Ay. My love.
The ship has sailed,
Suddenly and for ever.

Rosita leaned back in her chair and took another sip from her glass, letting the sound of the music spread through the channels carved out by the sherry.

She found herself pondering over Alba. As a young girl, Alba had sat giggling and squirming next to her on the benches of this very *taberna*. Now, heaven knows where she thought she was. Doña Rosita cast her mind back to her own wedding at which Alba had been chief bridesmaid, and then years later there was a picture of Alba as godmother, with Manuel holding their baby daughter and posing proudly for a photograph. And now here she was, sitting in the *taberna* alone, surrounded by young strangers who had their lives ahead of them. Rosita stared straight ahead, her square chin cupped in her left hand.

She was thinking about her best black fan in the wardrobe at home. She had bought it when she knew she was going to marry. At that time, the fan had been her most beloved possession because it was invested with all her hopes. It held all the promise of the future. She imagined how she would carry it as a married woman to fiestas and christening teas, wedding feasts and funerals, dances and birthday parties. And now, all that future was already past. Rosita's nose dripped and a tear fell on to her fingers as the guitar and the voice grew quieter and quieter until they finally stopped altogether.

From the audience, there was a unanimous gasp and moans of pleasure as the song faded into silence.

It occurred to Rosita that she must make sure her daughter had made proper plans for her burial, next to Manuel. Amidst the applause, yet another man took his place on the bench on the platform. He was a squat man of about thirty, his belly bursting over his jeans and with a face so fat that his eyes barely showed. He tuned his guitar a little and then launched into a beautiful, melancholy *solea*. The guitar unfolded bursts of heartbreaking melody alternating with a crashing, jangling tumult of chords.

By now the crowd was dense with people standing between

the tables. No one knew exactly how Doña Rosita squeezed to the front. She had the package under one arm and her bag in the other hand. The singer, immersed in his song, did not see her approach the stage. She climbed the three wooden steps on to the platform and stood there under the bright lights, never for a minute taking her attention from the singer, listening intently to every note. She put her belongings down on one side and walked slowly to the centre of the stage. The audience grew gradually quiet. In the background there was the clink of glasses being washed in the kitchen. The waiter, curious, stopped and leaned against the side wall, napkin over his arm, watching.

The singer realised he had company. Sitting on the bench, he turned towards Doña Rosita, nodded in acknowledgement and began to address his song to her.

She stood up straight, but with her head slightly lowered, entirely unaware of the audience, as if she were soaking in every word and note of the song through her skin. The stage was not large. The back wall against which she stood was built of plain limestone bricks. The bulky, but somehow humble, figure of Doña Rosita with her bow legs, in her black dress, not a silver hair out of place in the plaited knot at the back of her head, drew everyone's gaze.

Doña Rosita was clearly waiting. A feeling of anticipation gripped the spectators. She remained utterly still. The musician responded to the challenge of her stillness by making the chords of the guitar scream and slither down the scale until they were vibrating somewhere at the bottom. She did not move a muscle. The guitar tried to shake her into action, writhing, trembling, challenging, enticing her to break into motion. She remained immobile as if she had been there for centuries. Nothing happened. The musician sang another verse. She did not move. The crowd, which had been in an agony of suspense, thinking: Now, now, now she must move, became a little bored and then again thought: Now, now, it must be now, after which they lapsed into a sort of lull, as if they had joined her in this involuntary and timeless trance. The guitar music growled and grovelled and lapped at her feet trying to lure them into taking a step. The musician sang another couplet. Unexpectedly, the first, pale singer with the concave face stood up and repeated, in his lyrical alto voice, a single line of the same couplet.

In a split second and too fast for anyone to see, Doña Rosita broke out of the endless expanse of time, raised her arms, threw back her head and stamped her foot on the floor.

There was pandemonium. One man at a front table jumped to his feet to find that there were tears pouring down his face. He looked round:

'The *duende*,' he shouted, then pounded on the table and turned round to the audience with a gesture of triumph. 'You must have felt it. I feel twenty years younger.'

'The *duende* only appears at certain moments,' whispered the young student who had been sitting at Doña Rosita's table boasting to his girlfriend. He professed to know about such things. 'It's a gust of air, an irrepressible instant; a ghost suddenly appears and vanishes and the world is re-born.' Others were in the same state, throwing their programmes in the air. A sort of madness took hold of everybody. Strangers hugged one another. There were yells and whistles and the stamping of feet on the wooden boards of the floor lasted a full five minutes.

Doña Rosita went up, diffidently, to shake the hands

of the judges and collect her prize money. With that one gesture she had won the Taberna Verde's eighteenth dancing competition. The *taberna* was left in a furore.

She walked all the way home, a huge yellow moon sailing in the sky over her head. The night was warm. She travelled the four miles, through village after village, as if she were floating. Occasionally, a dog barked as she passed. She kept the packaged roll of green cloth tucked firmly beneath her arm.

When she reached her house, it was nearly midnight and her daughter and son-in-law stood outside with a knot of anxious neighbours.

'Where have you been?' Her daughter rushed towards her as Rosita slowly made her way up the hill towards their house. 'You must always tell us where you are going. We thought you had been called to your death.'

Rosita gave a grunting laugh.

She wished the neighbours good evening and apologised for any worry she had caused. Then she went inside the house, sensing that they were not ready to give up the novelty of their midnight worrying just because she had returned safely.

Behind the front door, she took off her shoes and felt, with relief, the cool tiles on her feet. She went upstairs and undressed. Before going to bed, she hid the prize money inside the roll of cloth on the top shelf of the wardrobe.

LUCIFER'S SHANK

Ellie arrived at about ten o'clock in the evening. I opened the door and she came in rolling her eyes and laughing with mock shivers at the extreme cold. Outside, a brisk wind blew. There were traces of frost on the neighbour's fence against a dark sky. She looked astonishingly alive. Her eyes were lively, her skin clear and her bush of black curls wiry and strong.

She had been reading Dante's *Inferno*, following the pilgrim's journey through the circles of Hell, with Virgil as his guide, and wanted to talk about it. Although she was absorbed in the work itself – reading a few cantos every night before going to sleep and finding it deeply satisfying – what had aroused her interest was the fact that this particular work of art had triggered off in her a series of powerful dreams. She had been trying to relate the different levels of the *Inferno* to her own dreams.

In the kitchen, she sat at the table, warming her hands round a mug of wild blackcurrant tea, talking intently, then pausing and frowning a little as she struggled to remember some of the images.

'There was something about fraud – the serpent becoming the man and vice versa. I can't remember exactly.'

She told me that, as the levels went lower and became hotter, she felt increasingly relaxed.

It had been her counsellor's idea that she should read some of the great works of literature. The woman had been quite specific in her recommendations and nearly all involved an epic journey of some sort. She had also suggested that Ellie visit an art gallery to look at one particular painting. I wish I could remember which one it was, but I've forgotten. What I do remember is Ellie returning from her visit to the gallery, excited and awestruck. It had been an inspired suggestion on the counsellor's part that such a secular and passionate woman as Ellie should turn for sustenance, at such a time, to literature and art.

She took off her scarf and hung her rust-coloured cardigan over the back of the chair.

'Have you got any honey to put in this tea?'

Her diet had already been altered to what she felt would give her the most nourishment and strength. The spoon tinkled in the cup. She went on talking.

'One of the "punishments" in the *Inferno* is to struggle against the wind.'

Then she told me how a few nights back she had dreamed that she was being buffeted by a violent wind as she struggled up a hill, knowing that to reach home would be to attain safety. But the wind hit her with body blows. There were clusters of other people, not exactly hostile, but not involved with her struggle, and she had to fight to move onward and upward. As she spoke I could feel the richness of whatever was beginning to take place inside her. Then she giggled.

'I'm farting a lot too with all this new diet of green stuff – so there's wind on the inside as well.'

We took our tea into the front room and sat on the floor as usual. Over the years, the floor had provided a magic carpet for the friendship. She was talking all the way. There had been another dream about her young son returning in a space capsule, his face white and waxen from the buffeting of re-entry. Someone pulled up his lids and looked in his eyes.

'It's all right, darling. You're alive,' she had said in the dream.

'Perhaps I was addressing the child in myself,' she commented.

We chatted about books and dreams and how she wanted to paint again. She wanted to make the best use of an unaccustomed luxury – time off from her teaching job.

'Oh, I know what,' I said, going over to the book-shelf. I took down *Is Nothing Sacred?* by Salman Rushdie. 'Let me read you some of this.'

We read the parts where he suggests literature and art in general be used as substitutes for religion. We talked about people we knew and how religion had made a mess of their lives. We talked about our political and secular beliefs and the importance of literature and how lucky we were to have access to it. How enriched.

'Yes. It's wonderful.' Ellie glowed with enthusiasm. We resolved to go and see some of the great theatre classics together. She said that she was going to read *Moby Dick* and then the *Odyssey*. And for some reason she wanted to visit Prague.

She spoke about the treatments and the drugs and how, after three treatments, she felt well. But most of all, she felt deeply alive, as if something were opening up inside her. She slept well too, utterly relaxed, open to profound dreams. She felt well.

Several years before, on a hot summer afternoon, we had gone to the cinema together in Notting Hill Gate. We were going to see an erotic Japanese film that we had both read about. I was greeted by her wild head of hair and broad grin as she waved through the window of my flat. She was wearing old blue jeans and a red T-shirt. Her Beetle car waited outside. She folded her long legs into the car, smacked the gears into place and drove off with her usual gusto.

When the film was over, we emerged from the cinema into a sultry London afternoon, shrieking with laughter at what a turn-on the film had been and how we should both rush to the nearest telephone box to phone a lover. Ellie was bent double in the street, wiping tears of laughter from her eyes. A warm, gritty breeze blew litter round our feet as we strolled back to the car, discussing the film seriously, each so interested in what the other had to say.

What can be better than going to the movies with a friend on a summer afternoon?

One winter's night years later, when she had had two children, it was firework night. I stood with Ellie and the kids on the edge of a crowd that had gathered to celebrate Guy Fawkes Night. A steely wind blew. The council had built a giant bonfire. Orange flames and sparks leapt into the black sky. For some reason those in charge had chosen 'The Ride of the Valkyries' to blare out from crackling speakers. There was something eerie and ominous about the large, silent crowd drained of life, circling the bonfire, facing the flames. Suddenly,

I had a premonition. Something terrible was going to happen.

'This is horrible,' I said to Ellie. 'It's like a warning.' She was leaning down, pulling her little girl's gloves on. I thought it was a warning about the holocaust; about the rise of racism in England; about empty and hypnotised crowds. I had a feeling of dread for the future.

The trouble with premonitions is that they sometimes attach themselves to the wrong event.

Why do we always try to cut people's tears off?

'Do you want a cup of tea?' I asked, as soon as I saw them welling up in her eyes. I ran with urgency through the hospital to a small canteen. A volunteer, an elderly woman with a sweet and vacant face, served me, too slowly, with a polystyrene cup full of watery tea.

It was August. I had come with Ellie to the hospital and sat at the back of the crowded clinic waiting for her to come out of the doctor's room. When she did come out, she looked like a different person, blind and not knowing where to go. She looked round in a daze. Suddenly, I realised that I would have to show her the way. She would need me to take her arm and be her guide. I got up and waved.

She had been clubbed on the back of the head with the words: 'It's not good, I'm afraid. It doesn't look good.'

We sat down at one side of the clinic while she sipped the tea and blinked back tears. There was another doctor that she had to see. This time I went in with her.

Dr Mackintosh was in his late thirties. His manner was quiet, firm and restrained as though he had been required to build up in himself an iron control against sorrow. Serious and attentive, he examined her and then explained in his soft Scots accent why he would recommend surgery immediately to remove her right breast. Yes, he nodded, she was welcome to come back when she had had time to register the news and he would answer any questions as best he could. No, it would not be wise to delay things for too long.

As he said goodbye at the door, I noticed that his brown hair was almost imperceptibly greying, as though it were brushed through with the grief of telling so many women that they had cancer. He was a rational doctor who would undoubtedly have smiled and said that his greying hair was due to genetic factors, just as he had told Ellie that her cancer had a genetic component. She arranged to come back and see him in five days.

'Dishy doctor,' she said with a woeful grin as we left the hospital.

Later that day at her house, drinking tea with the radio murmuring in the background, I was impressed by the speed with which she pulled herself together.

'I'm a very practical person,' she said as she fished around for scraps of paper on which she had written the addresses of self-help groups, alternative treatment centres, support groups, discussion groups, all given to her by the nurse at the hospital.

'I'll make some lists, just in case,' she said. And behind that list lay years of organising, political lobbying, supporting causes, demonstrations, letters of protest, all the apparatus and experience of trying to badger the world into being a better place.

I noticed, for the first time, that her wrists looked thin.

★   ★   ★

After the initial tears of shock, anxiety attacks, memories of her mother and the two purple holes of her mother's radical mastectomies, surreptitiously glimpsed in the bathroom when she was young; after the frozen inability to absorb the doctor's words, the fear of killing her mother with the news, concern about what to tell the children, talk of reconstruction, lymph glands, helplessly taking pamphlets about organisations, advice centres and drinking all that tea from polystyrene cups, she was worn out.

One day, before the operation, she went for a walk in Clissold Park. She lay down on the grass and fell asleep, exhausted, warmed by the September sun. Not knowing how long she had been asleep, she sat up. A young man with two children had stopped and was smiling down at her.

'Have you had a good sleep?' he asked.

'Wonderful, thank you.' She returned the smile. It was comforting. She felt that she was being watched over by a guardian angel.

Inside Dr Mackintosh's room once more, the window-blind flapped, obscuring the grimy hospital courtyard, as Ellie studied the list of questions she had prepared. She sat upright, her head inclined towards the paper in her hand, giving serious consideration to those questions which she thought most important to ask. A band of sunlight with motes of dust in it touched her fingers and the piece of paper. Something about her grace and dignity must have moved the doctor because he lowered his head for a moment before looking up and answering her question about the possibility of oedema after surgery.

★   ★   ★

We were in a side room of the ward when she showed me the scar. A bleak light came through the windows and fell on the sad, dark-green, plastic chairs. I was surprised and curious as she unwrapped herself and showed me the damage.

'You lucky thing,' I said. 'You look like Peter Pan. You've half managed to become a child again.' And it was true, the entirely flat side of her chest gave her that strange androgynous look of youth, as if time had been reversed. She laughed.

'I know what you mean,' she said. 'I quite like it.'

When I returned from abroad, she was halfway through her chemotherapy treatments.

It was summer. Ellie was going through a bad patch. The treatment had finished and the cancer had been halted. She started a flurry of angry verbal attacks on her boyfriend and their children.

The table was set in the garden. Douglas, her boyfriend, had put a bowl of African violets there which glimmered mauve in the dusk. All the rest of the garden flowers of that time of year, lupins, roses, wallflowers, sprawled unkempt and higgledy-piggledy in their beds or leaned out over the grass. We drank champagne. There were two other guests, a couple who lived down the road. Ellie felt mean and sour. Something deep and unstoppable made her niggle and push the knife in at every opportunity. The treatment was supposed to have eliminated the illness, but the anger went on.

Suddenly, she had an excruciating pain in her lower back. She became a whirlwind of destruction and hurled the paper plates at the fence.

'I want you to care for me,' she yelled at Douglas, 'provide for me, give me security, not sit in front of the television with a bottle of wine every night. Is this it?' She stood by the table, shouting. 'Is this all there is?'

They had been together since she was twenty. Now she was forty.

'I want out. I want my freedom.' Her face looked pinched. 'Is this all there is?' she screamed.

She phoned and wanted to come up. It was nine o'clock at night. She looked summery in a blue frock printed with sprigs of tiny white flowers, but also tired and a little drawn, having been back at work full-time since the beginning of term:

'I didn't sleep last night,' she said as we sat on the floor. 'My head was going round and round. I went to a meeting at the school about the government education cuts and I was so angry I couldn't sleep. I got up at the meeting and laid into the man, the apologist from the council. We had been sent a very clear leaflet spelling out what the cuts would mean. No music teacher. Can you imagine? No playground helpers – the ones that the timid kids always like to hang around.

'It was a brilliant meeting. The union guy said it was one of the best he's ever been to, even though he's an old hack. Anyway, I was so angry that I found myself shouting the council guy down. Up until then it had been polite questions and answers. I couldn't stand it any longer. I got up and said, it's a disgrace. I came here because of a very good leaflet. I didn't come here to hear you apologising and defeatist. I thought you would have suggestions, plans. That's why I'm here. I know about the cuts. I thought you would tell us what to do about them.

'I just let rip. You know, when I was about twenty I had an ambition to make a political speech and get a round of applause. Well, it took twenty years, but I got my round of applause. Then others joined in, enraged, confronting him. Teachers mainly. It was dynamite. I was waving my finger at him. I have to find something outside the home. I felt politically active. I felt that this was where I should be. I felt completely alive again.'

I nodded. From the start I had prepared myself for her death.

She came and sat on her usual side of the table in the kitchen. I made apricot tea, that delicious tea from the Algerian coffee shop in Soho. Again it was night, about nine o'clock after a cloudy summer's day. She had put on a little weight. Her features had rounded out. She looked rested, but the weight had swelled her remaining breast and she now suffered anguish at seeing the false breast in the mirror because it was too small and no longer a perfect match.

She had needed to buy a swimming costume for the holidays. She tried on some with padded cups. The cups were too pointed. The black woman assistant was so kind and soothing that she had nearly reduced Ellie to tears. Whichever costume she tried on, the scar showed and she wanted to retract herself from view. It made her want to cringe as if there was a hole in one side of her through which the wind might blow and set the exposed nerves aching. She felt vulnerable.

She stepped out of the shop into Oxford Street. There was nothing special about the day. It was a day much like any other except that she battled all the way home on the bus experiencing the misery of an irreversible deformity.

She had endured the same trauma whilst undergoing the radiotherapy treatment. An enormous lift took her down into the intestines of the hospital and the doors opened straight into the treatment room. There was no escape. She had to lie on the trolley bed while the ominous equipment was manoeuvred over her. Her arm was raised and with each treatment she felt the same agonising vulnerability. Her breast was gone and she shook with horror at the exposure of this voided torso to the machine.

'You know what I wanted to ask you,' she said, suddenly brushing the topic of illness aside. 'What do you think about this politician who's been having an affair with that actress? I was surprised last night, talking to a man who used to be an MP, that he seemed to think there should be legislation to protect privacy. But then, they tend to close ranks. But MPs are fair game. They choose public office. Anyway, these days it doesn't seem to make any difference. They're so corrupt they never resign anyway. Just carry on as though nothing had happened. But I don't think there should be laws to help them cover up what they do. They go on about family life and values and then create laws themselves that destroy poorer families.'

I agreed. She went on to talk about the way education was being undermined.

'Soon all the schools will have opted out from local authority government. They'll be managing themselves. And apparently, if they don't do well they'll be shut down. But what will happen to the children? I expect they'll do the same with the legal system soon. Value for money will be the criterion. Justice bounded by economics. Education and justice. Two things that seemed so absolute. Sold.'

Flitting through my mind as she spoke were thoughts about all the meetings she had attended: meetings with staff;

meetings with students; meetings with her women's group to discuss issues or read poetry or study paintings or photographs; meetings to arrange a rota of help for a sick friend; meetings on local issues such as the noise made by the re-building of Arsenal football stadium; helping with school events; taking poor city kids for weekends in the country.

The tea became lukewarm in its dark-blue enamel teapot. We embraced and she left. She would be on holiday for a month in France.

At the end of that month, a friend from South America arrived to study in England. Ellie had been one of several people who had paid something towards his fare. She opened the door of her house and greeted him with such warmth that he stood transfixed on the doorstep and nearly melted.

That evening she sat at the table laden with the meal's debris, the remnants of Douglas's cooking, joints of pork, chicken, green salads gleaming with oil and garlic dressing, half-empty bottles of wine, and she listened with delight to stories of life in the bush. He, in turn, was mesmerised by her radiant attention. But at about ten o'clock she began to flag and eventually excused herself because she was feeling suddenly exhausted even though the cancer had gone and she was in full remission.

The phone rang. It sounded like someone with a bad cold. It was not a cold. It was the result of crying. Ellie was ringing from the hospital. The cancer had come back. It was in the hip, leg and the throat. Ellie was distraught, sobbing.

'I want to see my children grow up.'

A short while later she rang me again, sounding in control of herself.

'We'll just have to do it all over again,' meaning, I presumed, the chemotherapy, and the fight in general.

I went round to her house. Ellie arrived about a quarter of an hour later and we both behaved too normally – as if what had been discovered was nothing more than a blasted nuisance, an inconvenience like a car breakdown. The children watched television in the front room.

Douglas came home. She sat at the kitchen table with him and told him.

'Oh Ellie,' he said sympathetically, 'you shouldn't have to go to those places on your own.' He looked down. He could rarely bear to go with her. They talked sensibly, hands touching firmly and gently.

That night we went up to her room, Ellie and I. The children were in bed. Douglas was watching television.

Ellie had always wanted a deep, rose-pink carpet. Now it was a bit worn but still retained a soft glow in the lamplight. The bed was half made, books and papers scattered on it. The bedside lamp shone on another pile of books on the chest of drawers beside the bed.

'It's a funny thing,' she said, 'just last night I started looking at Dante's *Inferno* again. Do you remember how I used to read it and get such a lot from it?' She picked up a paperback of *The Divine Comedy*. 'I was reading the part where they are climbing down Lucifer's shank.'

She lowered herself gingerly on to the bed with the book in her hand and started to search for the passage. 'There are two versions. One has them climbing down Lucifer's shaggy body, reaching the thigh and turning themselves upside-down so that they start to climb up his legs. In the other version, a different translation, Lucifer himself turns upside-down.'

She handed me the book and levered herself awkwardly off the bed again to find the second version. My heart sank as I looked through the canto. Why had she chosen that image? Lucifer, a thousand feet tall, his body piercing the centre of the earth, winged with featherless wings like those of a bat. I read the first section she had pointed out:

> And thus from shag to shag descended down
> Twixt matted hair and crusts of frozen rime.
> And when we came to where the huge thigh-bone
> Rides in the socket at the haunches' swell,
> My guide, with labour and great exertion
> Turned head to where his feet had been and fell
> To hoisting himself up upon the hair.

How would we ever overcome such images? She stood by the bed puzzling over the two texts. It seemed that there was a way out, that by climbing Lucifer's shank they reached the River Lethe as a small stream and by following it upwards they could gaze towards an opening where the stars appeared, and so they journeyed, against the flow of the stream, against oblivion and towards recollection. It was this path she was looking for and she was using Dante's *Divine Comedy* as her street guide.

I shuddered. The giant shaggy thigh of Lucifer with its hanks of frozen goat hair. It was too powerful.

With some difficulty, she struggled into a nightie and lay down on top of the duvet with its gay pattern of geometrical shapes in bright colours. I looked down at her long limbs, beautifully arranged on the bed. There was no sign of anything wrong. Despite the pain in her right hip and leg, when she managed to lie down on the bed the limbs looked strong and well-proportioned with no sign of the ravages taking place inside.

The next day she was washing dishes in the kitchen when the pain exploded with threefold ferocity. A young, pony-tailed nurse from the pain team arrived and prescribed morphine. The pain was in the socket of her right thigh-bone and hip. Exactly where the turning point of Dante's journey took place. She could hobble with a stick but if anything jarred the leg she suffered agonies that left her white-faced and immobile. Her eyes seemed so enormous and blue in that ashen face. Later they found that her hip-bone had fractured in its socket and they gave her an operation to replace it immediately. The cancer was in the bones.

Cancer always seemed to me to have something to do with the sea, not just because of the name, cancer the crab, a creature whose direction is unpredictable, which comes at you sideways and unexpectedly. There are other connections with water. I have an image of swimming in a blue sea and catching sight of the undulating shadows of black rocks beneath the surface, menacing, ominous. After I swim away, the shapes disappear. The sea is brilliantly clear, the sky wide, the coast distant. And then, suddenly, there they are again, the shapes.

Gradually, Ellie struggled to walk again with the hip replacement. She walked the length of a shopping centre and triumphantly bought a scarlet cotton dress with a low neck and tiny black pattern. Back in her house, she tried it on while I sprawled on the bed. She stood in front of the full-length mirror and adjusted the sleeves.

'Yes. I like it,' she said approvingly. And the vibrant colour did suit her as she turned this way and that, studying the mirror's image.

The next day, we visited the consultant. Often, on those visits, I felt less like a friend than a grim guard, escorting someone relentlessly to their execution. Using a stick, she gripped my arm. I had to hold up the traffic with one hand because she took such a long time to cross the road. Despite the pain-relief team, she was in constant agony.

The consultant's clinic was crowded and noisy. She pointed out a hand-written notice that said '200 more managers – 200 less beds!!!' and pulled a face. When her name was called we went into a small room that barely kept out the sounds of the busy clinic outside. She was no longer seeing Dr Mackintosh. It was not even the same hospital. This consultant was dark, charming, suave, informal and vague. As we entered, he complained wearily that the increase in bureaucratic paperwork made him spend less time with his patients.

Ellie pulled out another list of questions. He listened and answered sympathetically. The disease was unpredictable. 'The aim is to control the tempo of it. The hope is that it will be containable. Sometimes it goes haywire and then we can't contain it.'

'What . . . what . . . what sort of . . . How . . .' Nearly in tears, she looked over to me for help.

'She wants to know how long she has got to live,' I said,

feeling strangely brutal and recognising the uncomfortable pleasure of knowing that the question did not refer to me.

'Do I have six months?' she asked.

'That's the most difficult question we're always asked.' He looked out of the window for a moment, then raised his shoulders, swivelled round in his chair to face us and opened his arms.

'I'd stick my neck out and say yes. I will give you Oromorph to control the pain. You can take as much as you need.'

She found some hope for recovery in his words. I did not. He gave himself away in those few seconds when he looked out of the window.

On the way back, she sat in front with the Greek mini-cab driver, a man in his fifties whom she could not resist lecturing on the iniquities of the Conservative government and their policies on public transport and the health service while she took the occasional swig of liquid morphine.

It was in the early hours of the morning. The telephone by my bed rang. I lifted it up and an extraordinarily deep, masculine voice growled, 'It's me.'

The voice was an octave lower than most human voices. It sounded like a voice from one of those old-fashioned, turn-handle gramophones when the record is slurring and getting slower and deeper as it winds down.

'I don't know what . . . I can't . . . I don't . . .'

'Is that you, Ellie?'

'Yes.' Then came the sound of teeth chattering at an abominable volume, like the clattering of dishes.

'What's happened?'

'I'm fr . . . I'm frightened.'

'Is Douglas there?'

'I c . . . can't speak to him,' came the reply, riddled with hiccups. 'Y . . . you s . . . said I could phone y . . . you any time.'

The slow voice roller-coasted up and down. I sat up sleepily in bed and felt myself recoiling in horror from her fear. I wanted to hang up. Instead, I started to talk chattily about what I had been doing that day. All the time, I was desperate for the conversation to end. She replied occasionally, sounding as if she were speaking from the bottom of some cavernous pit. I began to talk her up as if she were a climber who had fallen to a ledge halfway down the cliff face with no safety net.

Then I had a bright idea.

'You know what has happened, Ellie? You know why you're feeling like this?' I was determined to make this the truth.

'Whaat?' The voice was sounding more normal.

'It's the drugs. The drugs are making you feel so strange. You're full of morphine. That's why you're feeling weird. That's the only reason. You're perfectly all right. The drugs are making you feel like that.'

'Do you think so?'

'I'm sure. I'm positive.' I was willing it to be the truth.

'Perhaps I shouldn't take so much.' The voice was sounding up to speed. The tone had risen to a more normal pitch.

'Do you think you'll be able to sleep now?'

'Yes. I'm feeling better. Thanks.'

We talked on for a little until I could feel sleep settling on her. We said goodbye and I hung up. I felt sick.

★   ★   ★

Some hours later, when it was still dark, I woke to find a tall dark woman, full of sorrow, standing at the bottom right-hand corner of the bed. The hair was in a straight bob. She looked familiar. She wore dark cothes and was drowned in sadness. I struggled to wake up properly and swung my feet out of the bed to put them on the floor. I looked up and there was nobody there. When I thought about the figure later, I sensed that the woman had been some sort of combination of Ellie and myself. I suppose it must have been a dream but it felt real.

That summer, Ellie held a birthday party in her garden. She held court from an elongated garden chair like a *chaise-longue*, wearing a straw hat with flowers round the brim. The garden was crammed with friends, children and food. Ellie looked well and happy, opening presents and talking to the children. But all of us felt that the future had been foreshortened in some way.

I drove at furious speed towards the hospital, maddened by the dawdling of the other traffic which did not even attempt to jump the lights. I had received a call from Douglas telling me to get there fast. There was no parking space in the underground hospital car-park. I drove round and round the gloomy, subterranean area with its hollow sounds, agonising over the waste of time until someone pulled out and I shot into their place.

The day before, Ellie had gone into a hospice for a week's respite care, to relax and have some tests. The next morning she had got out of bed and fallen. The other leg had snapped and broken.

An ambulance had brought her to this hospital. I ran

through the dark corridors looking for the fracture clinic. To my relief I came across two of Ellie's friends, sitting on a bench outside the swing doors of the operating theatre. A nurse came out and to our surprise we were allowed into the white, arctic waste of dazzling walls and lights where Ellie lay having her leg bound from thigh to ankle in wet plaster of paris. A nurse from the hospice stroked her forehead.

'Oh Ellie, you poor thing,' I commiserated. 'At least it's not the same leg as before.'

She opened her eyes and rolled them with that familiar look of weary exasperation.

'Talk about "Aw me bliddy leg",' I said. It was a private joke. When her other hip fractured, I had given her a fist-sized hand-painted stone. The picture showed a house at night with one light on in the top window and 'Aw me bliddy leg' written in a balloon coming from the lighted window.

'Yes. It's "Aw me bliddy leg" all right,' she said, smiling before drifting off again.

Jokes. What a rackety handrail to help us through the blizzard.

I found Ellie's room at the hospice rather spartan and functional although she had seemed quite satisfied with it. Two days after her broken leg was plastered she lay propped on pillows in a coma. Just before she went into the coma she had made a gargantuan effort to sit up in bed, frowning with concentration, bewilderment and determination, struggling to remain in the land of the living. Friends helped her to lie back again. Family and friends came and went and chatted round the bed. They say that hearing is the last thing to go. I worried that she could hear what people were saying about her death. There was not much noise apart from the regular rattle of the machine that automatically shot morphine into her veins.

I watched.

According to some groups of South American Indians, it is the manner of death, the way that you die, that determines your after-life, not the sort of life you have led, and I can see the truth in that. The real self is revealed only in death.

In those last few days, I saw the earth gradually claiming my friend back. For Ellie and me, the last coherent exchange had been a shared joke. She was transmuting into clay. Her face was heavy and drawn down by gravity. The elasticity of the waxen skin altered and thickened like Plasticine and her features seemed to go through several different stages of being almost weighted and pulled into shapes by G-forces. Each day there was a different configuration of features. Death is related to the force of gravity.

Eventually, and unexpectedly, a strikingly beautiful empress took up her position on the bed with an expression of relaxed and heavy disdain. A tragic sensuality emerged, the bloom of power weighted with the burdens of dictatorship. The politics, values and activities of a lifetime had nothing to do with this. This was another self come true, the self that could have been. She lay there with a magnificence that I had never seen or understood before. It belonged to the certainty of no longer dealing with exchange, interaction or give and take. Life is the mask that drops off and death protrudes from underneath as the reality – a reality which has been long hidden by disguise. The masquerade was over.

It is never possible to pin down the moment of death with accuracy, even if the most recent atomic measuring clock were to hand. It does not take place at one instant. The event is a blurring of boundaries, a smudge, indefinable, a mystery. At what point do you measure the last exhalation, the last movement of the blood, the heart's final tremor, which brain cell fires after all the rest. The change is gradual and extraordinary and usually imperceptible. You are never quite sure when it has happened. A little while before Ellie died her eyes opened and stared at nothing, beautiful glazed grey-blue eyes, lolling like heavy blooms on stalks.

She died on firework night, five years to the day after I had experienced that premonition. The first sporadic rockets exploded in the night sky as I made my way home. The premonition had been misplaced, although I suppose that each individual death is in some way its own holocaust.

DON'T GIVE ME
YOUR SAD STORIES

All laughter is either triumphant or helpless and Jimmy McLeod was in need of the latter variety. That's why he was looking for Dave. Whenever Jimmy wanted a certain sort of drinking companion he tried to track down Dave Garner. Dave would help him get rid of the tension. It was early Sunday evening. The Soho pub was half dead. Jimmy went over to the telephone by the bar and dialled the number of Dave's ex-wife. A woman answered. Jimmy held the receiver away from his ear a bit so he didn't have to listen to the thin voice complaining about how she'd been divorced from Dave for two years but that he still insisted on coming round for his Sunday dinner. There was a long pause, then Dave's voice came on the line.

'How's the crack?' Jimmy enquired.

'I was sleeping, as it happens.' The voice sounded dozy and slow like a cat purring.

'I don't know why Eileen puts up with you.'

'Oh I just like to bring me laundry here on a Sunday for old time's sake.' The two men giggled. 'Anyway, don't you understand, I'm a sort of status symbol. People come round here and they see me asleep on the sofa, all bevvied, snoring, one sock on and one sock off, and they think: Christ! It must cost fifty quid a day to keep him in that state.'

Jimmy laughed. He felt better already. The woman with untidy hair behind the bar smiled over at him.

'Are you coming up or what?' Jimmy was frowning now, anxious in case Dave couldn't make it.

'Where are you?'

'The Three Grapes.'

'Fucking hell. I can't come there. The other night I sold some of the prostitutes a whole lot of nylon stockings with no feet. There was a little altercation. My popularity rating has slumped in that hostelry and you know how sensitive I am.' Jimmy relaxed at the sound of Dave's chuckle. 'Go over to The Tin Pan Alley and I'll meet you there.'

'I can't stand that place,' said Jimmy fiercely. 'It's full of depressing fucking drinkers. I like happy drinkers.'

'Go to The Bells then, Quasimodo. And you will soon be joined by Davido Garneroni, ice-cream millionaire and laughter merchant. If anyone comes near us with a long face, we'll batter them. Give me an hour. I want to go home and change first.'

Jimmy had forgotten how fastidious Dave was about his cheap clothes. 'Get a move on then.'

Jimmy put the phone back on the hook. He felt easier now that he knew Dave would be joining him. Sunday evenings always made him edgy, lonely but without wanting to talk to anybody. The pubs were always flat at this hour on a Sunday. He ordered a pint of house ale and took it over to the table by the door. He sat facing the door. He never drank with his back to the door. His mouth was still dry from last night. He sipped the beer. The door banged to and fro letting in warm air as the evening's custom built up. Two blonde prostitutes sauntered in for a drink before work. Both wore short skirts and leather jackets, one had lipstick the colour of pig's liver. They perched on bar stools. A minute later the doorman from the clip-joint next door joined them.

'It's a fact, though. They always like blondes on a Saturday, for some reason,' he was saying.

'Yeah, well, it's fucking Sunday, remember?' hissed one of the girls.

Jimmy wondered if Danny Kennedy would show up. He was one of the few people Jimmy could tolerate when he was in this sort of a mood. Danny was a seaman. He used this pub when he was on shore leave. He had a quiet sense of humour. Last time they had drunk together, Danny had missed his ship. Dave Garner was altogether different. Dave had the tongue of an angel. He could spin a tale out of anything. That was Dave's gift – seduction by story.

The warm beer did not do much for the nervous churning of Jimmy's stomach. He lit a cigarette. Something had happened last night. Small scraps of skin were missing from his knuckles. He must have punched something. A door, maybe. He couldn't remember. He had woken up at half-past four in the morning in a pedestrian precinct, not knowing where he was. It had all looked less familiar than anywhere he had ever seen. He was lying on a cold paved concourse. He'd got up and shaken himself down, then started to walk. In the grey light of early morning, he recognised nothing. The wide street was deserted, the imposing buildings totally unfamiliar. He was in a foreign city. He walked all the way down the Strand convinced that he was in Sydney, Australia. Jesus Christ, how in hell's name did I get here, he thought in horror. It was not until Trafalgar Square came into sight ten minutes later that he understood, breaking into a sweat of relief, that he was still in London.

That was Dave's other gift. He could keep up with Jimmy's drinking.

'Do you think we have a drink problem?' Dave asked once. 'I'd join Alcoholics Anonymous but I can't stand the anonymity.' They both fell around laughing.

The last time he had actually seen Dave was two years ago. Jimmy had gone up to Liverpool with Scotch Eddy and Dave for Dave's uncle's funeral. They had all known Dave's uncle as 'The Windswept Rabbit' because he wore a fake-fur-collar coat and his eyes protruded a little due to a thyroid condition. He had acquired the nickname on a cold, windy day which he had spent stuffing towels down pub toilets, so that they overflowed, and then offering his services as a plumber to the publican. One of the publicans had discovered the trick and pulled a gun on him. It was the way he had hopped out of the pub, darting from side to side in case of bullets, that got him his nickname. The Windswept Rabbit always drank with them whenever he passed through London.

'All right, Mary? Sorry about the Rabbit'n that,' said Jimmy awkwardly when they arrived. Jimmy was wearing a grey suit. What he called his 'suit of no smiles'. The suit for a no-smile situation.

'Yeah, well, I don' know where he's gone but wherever it is I hope there's a letter box for his giro,' said Mary, wife of the deceased. She stood in the parlour in a leopard-skin, wrap-around top and a black skirt, her scalp and hair hennaed red. The parlour had thin brown carpet on the floor and was bare but for the sofa, the television set and a formica-topped metal table surrounded by four plastic chairs. She handed out cans of lager to the dozen odd mourners who had assembled.

'He was dead choked, the day before he died,' continued Mary, 'because some dwarf won the Best First-comers singing competition in the pub. He thought he should have won. I don't know why, because with that hole in his throat he could hardly speak, never mind sing. But he'd been practising for ages.'

The Windswept Rabbit had been suffering from cancer of the throat. Whenever the nurse came to change the dressing, she found a note pinned on the front door telling her to come and change the bandages at Yates's Wine Lodge.

'Was it the cancer that killed him like?' asked Scotch Eddy nervously. None of them knew much funeral etiquette.

'Oh no,' said Mary. 'He went to the lavvy and pulled the chain and the cistern fell down on his head.'

The room gradually filled with cigarette smoke, chatter and the subdued spurting of cans of lager being opened. There was a discussion as to whether it was legal to cash the Rabbit's latest giro.

'You can cash it,' wheezed one of the mourners. 'Giros are a week in hand. So he's still owed it even if he's dead.'

'Ah well,' said the Rabbit's brother, after an hour or so, 'I might as well be off. Gotta get back to work and anyway, none of his suits fit me.' Everybody laughed. He downed his lager, paid his respects once more and left. His departure started the exodus. Feeling that it was OK to leave for jollier premises, Jimmy, Scotch Eddy and

Dave said their goodbyes and went drinking in the centre of town.

Jimmy had told Dave not to do it.

'You're too drunk,' he'd said. 'I'm not going with you. You won't make it. We're all too pissed.'

'Watch me. I'm magic,' crowed Dave. They were standing on the pavement outside Yates's Wine Lodge. A light drizzle had wet Dave's wavy black hair, making a strand of it fall across his eyes which were alight with excitement.

From the other side of the road they winced as they watched him, drunk as a skunk, weave his way through the traffic and into the ground-floor jewellery department of a large store. Three minutes later, he emerged through the swing doors, smiling beatifically, carrying a tray of diamond rings, with one glittering necklace over his left ear and two shop assistants hanging on to his arms. Almost simultaneously, the police van drew up. There was a small but unseemly scuffle. The assistants retrieved their gems and two policemen grabbed Dave, one by each arm, running him towards the van. Dave tripped. The two police tripped with him. They all bowed forward. The three of them, arms linked, dipped and recovered their balance in perfect formation and Dave, skipping forward with his two partners, began to sing in an encouraging, tuneful voice, 'We're off to see the Wizard, the wonderful Wizard of Oz.'

Jimmy and Scotch Eddy watched him dancing into the van.

'No point in us all getting done for conspiracy,' Scotch Eddy muttered, and they'd caught the train back to London.

Jimmy heard from Dave once in the two years. They had sent him to an open jail somewhere in Cumbria. The letter was neatly written and complained at length about a Mr Edwards in the welfare department. Apparently, Mr Edwards had asked Dave whether his wife was in need of extra blankets. 'Who does he fucking think we are,' fumed Dave. 'Let him stick his own wife under grotty welfare blankets. We are a DUVET family.' Once in a misplaced fit of idealism, Mr Edwards had tried to engage Dave in a rehabilitative conversation. Acknowledging his undoubted intelligence, Mr Edwards had spoken to Dave about Edmund Burke and the idea of the social contract. 'Ah, but I never fucking signed it,' Dave had replied, grinning. There was more in his letter about how he had been thrown off the carpentry course after a minor ruck with a man called Oil-Can Harry. It seemed that Oil-Can Harry was definitely up for the slash-cut-and-run treatment if Dave encountered him again on the outside.

The clock on the pub wall pointed to half-past seven. Another twenty minutes and Jimmy would go and meet Dave. He flexed his right hand. It was painful and stiff after smashing into whatever it had smashed into the night before. He might not be able to go to work in the morning. The thought pleased him and troubled him at the same time. He liked to work and then . . . sometimes he liked to let it all go. When he did work it was as a steeplejack. Steeplejacking was about the only work he could tolerate in London. That way he could get up and out of the city. He had no fears of the great heights. He could walk along bouncing narrow planks hundreds of feet up and not feel even a shiver of apprehension. He loved the freedom and detachment he experienced seeing the city spread out far beneath him. It was only up there that he felt truly relaxed.

He'd got Dave a job with him once. Dave lasted a day. He spent the whole time on the ground giving the foreman a load of flannel about a slipped disc. Heights didn't suit Dave. He belonged on the ground or under it – trotting in and out of the dark warren of dive-bars and underground drinking holes like a pit pony. Dave's preferred exercise was swinging the lead. Jimmy needed to be able to see horizons – any horizon, an ocean, a desert, distant mountains. He preferred landscapes without people.

Someone put Nat King Cole's 'Honeysuckle Rose' on the juke-box and the pub shook into a languid sort of life. Jimmy stubbed out his cigarette. As he looked up, an unwelcome sight hove into view. Fat Roger, belly flying at half-mast, bustled towards him, clutching a half-pint of beer that slopped over his hand as he walked. He looked more than somewhat frantic.

'That pillock of a magistrate. Did you hear what he did? He bound us all over to keep the peace.' Roger sat, uninvited, opposite Jimmy. He smelt of stale biscuits and his moist lips quivered like those of a gerbil.

'He binds the Grants over. Fair enough. They started it. Then he binds me over and the wife and the kids, all of us, the whole family! That's out of order.'

Apparently, there has been some fracas in the street involving Fat Roger and his neighbours. Fat Roger launched into a long saga of music being played too loud; washing disappearing from the line; stones being thrown at the dog; exchanges of insults; overthrown dustbins and finally, a flurry of fisticuffs on the pavement. Jimmy listens to the whining voice with mounting distaste. Nat King Cole turns into the Bee Gees who gotta getta letta to somebody and Fat Roger spots that Jimmy is about to try and leave and changes tack. He pulls out a roll of cartridge paper from under his arm.

'Do you like this? I've taken up painting.' He unfurls a picture of something that might be a railway siding.

'That's terrific, Roger.' Jimmy lifts his jacket from the back of the chair and stands up.

'Paddy Lennon's in hospital.' Fat Roger makes a last-ditch attempt to detain him.

'Oh yeah?' Jimmy pauses a second too long and misses his exit. Fat Roger's eyes gleam with triumph.

'You remember Rosemary, his bird, the one with the poppy-out eyes who swallows pills the whole time? Well, they're in bed one night and she's depressed. So she sits up and starts moaning on and on and Paddy's trying to sleep so he takes no notice. And then she starts to scratch at her wrists with a razor. So she pokes him in the back and tells him she's cut her wrists. Well, he still takes no notice. So she cuts his wrists. Hahahahahahaha.' The story seems to cheer Fat Roger up.

'I'm off to try and find Dave Garner,' says Jimmy gruffly.

'Where is he? He owes me a tenner. Where will you be?' The whining voice follows Jimmy to the door.

'If I knew where I'd be, I wouldn't go there.' Jimmy is about to go through the door when a heavily built man with a face like an eighteen-pound hammer comes in. He walks in slowly, like a sleepwalker, hardly aware of his surroundings. He's wearing a collarless shirt and a raincoat.

Fat Roger's eyes light up at the thought of company: 'Hello there, Frank.'

The man looks up, registers Fat Roger and moves sombrely towards the table.

Jimmy makes his escape. The pub doors bang to and fro behind him.

Outside, it is still light. A blue silk sky runs into the jagged rooftops. Jimmy clenches his teeth. From Luigi's bakery, the smell of Monday's freshly baked bread is already hitting the street reminding him that he hasn't eaten. Whisky will cure him of his appetite. The restless feeling still has hold of him and there is a tension at the back of his head. He passes Harry's Rehearsal Bar and crosses over past the dive bar at the end of Gerrard Street and into The Bells.

Dave is already there, standing with his back to the bar. His is the smile of a dissolute priest. He has captured a dupe, a gullible-looking man with spectacles and a mackintosh. Catching sight of Jimmy, he winks.

'Oi-oi, Crazy-Horse. Come and meet my new pal. This man,' he says with apparent deference, 'is a writer. What is it you write exactly?'

'Adaptations mainly,' says the man, falling into the trap. 'I've just adapted a Trollope for the BBC.'

'Have you indeed? Was that problematic? I always find a little trollop is fine unless you happen to be dealing in stockings with no feet.' Dave's laugh gurgles up through his catarrh. The man tries to conceal his puzzlement. Jimmy gets the drinks in.

'This is my mate, Crazy-Horse.'

'Hi,' says the man, unable quite to bring himself to say 'Crazy-Horse'.

'We're the salt of the earth. Isn't that right, Jimmy?'

'Aye. The Sifta twins.' Jimmy raises his glass and downs the smooth, sharp whisky.

'What do you do?' The man asks Dave.

'Me? I'm third-generation unemployed from Liverpool and I'm fully expecting to pass on the business to my son.' Dave's mood is expansive and genial. Jimmy has seen him otherwise, delivering punches with the strength of an ox.

'That must be rough.' The man peers sympathetically from behind his spectacles, 'Being unemployed.'

'Rough? It's a tragedy. I have to sit on the tube in the morning with a packet of sandwiches so it looks as if I've got a job. When I was a kid, the cockroaches formed a union and struck for better conditions. I think it's your round.'

Jimmy and Dave order doubles.

'It must be nice to be a writer, an intellectual.' Dave sounds wistful.

'It's not all roses,' says Mr Gullible. 'It's bloody hard work, sitting down all day, trying to get a word right, trying to get an idea.'

'How much do they pay you for sitting down all day trying to get an idea?' Dave enquires innocently.

'Well, the BBC doesn't really pay too well. A grand or two in advance, maybe . . .'

Jimmy interrupts, as Dave knew he would.

'Just a minute there. I've been hanging on to a brick chimney-stack, two hundred-odd feet in the air, repairing it in a high wind for four pounds an hour. That makes a man sort of philosophical.' There is a hint of menace in his voice. 'I've noticed something in life. You can't pretend to be a steeplejack. You can pretend to be a writer. But you can't pretend to be a steeplejack. You have to do it. If you don't do it well, you get your cards. They don't pay you while you're "on pause". I suspect that you are a comma, waiting to be a full stop.'

The man looks discomfited.

'Ah, but you're not a writer, are you, pal?' chimes in Dave the disingenuous. 'You're just an adaptor, if I'm not mistaken.'

The man rises to it and begins to bluster.

'It's quite a craft, you know.'

'Oh it's a craft, is it?' Jimmy leans towards him and the man cannot tell threat from twinkle. 'Well, in my trade you would be what is known as a labourer's labourer, the lowest of the low.' Jimmy can smell the man's musk after-shave. There is a pulse beating in the writer's throat. 'Have you got any idea of the amount of thought that goes into creating a brick? Never mind your Trollopes and your Tolstoys. Did you know that the hole in a brick is called a "frog"? Do you know who first designed this marvellous thing we call a BRICK?'

'No.' The man's eyes are flitting towards Dave for help which is not forthcoming.

'Neither do I.' Jimmy lets out a joyous hoot of laughter and slaps him on the back. The man makes his excuses and leaves.

'I love winding people up,' says Dave. 'Where shall we go now?'

An hour later, they are sitting in the maroon flock gloom of Harry's Rehearsal Bar. Musack seeps out from speakers on the wall. Dave gives the speakers a suspicious stare.

'Is that music or are they trying to gas us?' he says as he

rolls a cigarette. Sitting in one of the booths is an ageing blonde with her hair in a French pleat. Her name is Susan Shanks. That's where she always sits. Rumour has it that she was a famous film star. The name always seems to ring a bell but nobody remembers the films.

Jimmy and Dave are seated in another alcove getting steadily drunk. Conversation is intense.

Says Jimmy, 'If there's one thing I hate more'n anything, it's people who come up to me when I'm pissed and start telling me their sad stories. There I am, trying to have a nice time, and some Hoo Chief Duper comes up to me and tells me that his wife has left him or he's dying of cancer of the arsehole or his hands got caught in the cement mixer and he'll never be able to play the piano again.' Jimmy's grimace of dislike contains a hint of violence. 'Why don't they understand? I don't care. I really don't fucking care. Why do they always tell me crab stories? And I'm trying to be all nice to them. What I really want to say is "Bollocks".'

Jimmy is beginning to enjoy that feeling of mounting hilarity that a couple of hours in Dave's company usually induces. Dave picks up the theme like a jazz musician, offering his variation.

'Don't tell me it happens to you too.' He puts his hands on his hips mimicking a gossip. 'I thought it was just me. I thought I was the only one they picked on, the no-hopers, the doom and disaster brigade. Look at that dog.' The club-owner's dog is staring sadly up at them from in front of the bar. 'He's one of them.'

Jimmy tries focusing his eyes to consider the dog.

'Either that or he's secretly trying to hypnotise us into buying him a drink.'

They are both laughing now, mellow.

'That being said,' says Jimmy, 'have you got Evostick on your arse or are you going to get us something to drink?'

Dave comes back with more drinks. He is just putting two shots of whisky on the table when there is a draught from the door and Fat Roger appears out of nowhere. He is accompanied by the collarless man with a face like an eighteen-pound hammer. Fat Roger is looking shifty.

'All right, Jimmy? All right, Dave? Can't stop now. Look after my mate Frank for a bit till I get back.' And he's gone.

'That's funny.' Dave raises his eyebrows. 'Our Roger doesn't usually disappear when there's a little light refreshment to be imbibed.'

'Or when he's owed a tenner,' says Jimmy. 'Sit down, cha. What'll you have?' The man joins them at the table. Jimmy returns from the bar with three drinks.

'Did I tell you about the potatoes this morning?' Dave kicks off with a story about two pounds of Edward's potatoes tumbling from a hole in his pocket in the underground train that morning, while he sat trying to look as if nothing unusual was happening. Jimmy is chortling. The other man manages a ghost of a smile. Jimmy and Dave exchange glances. Dave spins another yarn that involves a five-pound note, a box and a rat. The man's face doesn't move a muscle.

'It seems to me,' says Dave, 'that my stories are falling upon stony ground.'

'Pebbles,' says Jimmy.

'Shale,' says Dave.

'Shingle,' says Jimmy.

'It seems to me that my stories are being sucked out to sea on a receding tide.'

Jimmy strikes a pose and addresses the man.

'Excuse me, Mr Whoever You Are. Either smile or FUCK OFF.'

Heads at the bar turn. The man's eyes remain fixed on his drink. His shoulders sag and a look of apologetic despair crosses his face.

'Sorry about this, folks. It's difficult to explain.' He speaks as though he was been winded. All he can muster is a whisper. 'My fifteen-year-old son hung himself in the kitchen yesterday.'

Jimmy shoots backwards in his seat, staring at the man with a look of horrified exasperation. Dave is looking at the man as if he has just done something offensive, like fart. There is silence at the table. Then Jimmy hears what sounds like the distant screaming whistle of an approaching train. The noise is coming from inside him. He glances at Dave. Dave's shoulders are shaking. Jimmy's face screws up in an effort to suppress what he has been waiting for all evening and what has finally arrived. He clenches the muscles at the bottom of his stomach, fighting to keep it down. Then his cheeks fill with air and the laughter explodes upwards and outwards with the force of a first oil strike in the desert, black gold spurting and bubbling skywards. He leans backwards, roaring. Tears of helpless laughter blur his vision. Dave is in paroxysms on the other side of the table. Their companion stares straight ahead towards the door.

THE PARROT
AND DESCARTES

I had better tell you about the parrot.

In the Orinoco region, it is said, everything began with a wish and a smell. A hand stuck up out of the earth. An arm. The earth opened. A woman who was watching turned into a male parrot and began to scream a warning. Then all sorts of things happened. A man dropped a gourd of urine, scorching his wife's flesh with it. Her skin was roasted. Her bones fell apart. Night burst over the world and something white like a capuchin monkey went running into the forest. That's what they say. I wasn't there myself.

Centuries later, still in a state of shock, the same parrot that had screamed the warning was discovered in a guava tree by a certain Sir Thomas Roe. Sir Thomas was an English courtier, known as Fat Thom, who travelled up the Orinoco in 1611. He pulled back some foliage and discovered the bird, amongst the leaves, head on one side, returning his gaze with curiosity. The parrot was green. At first Fat Thom thought that sunlight was falling on the bird's head, then he saw that it had a golden beak. In other words the creature was a traditional plain and not particularly fancy South American parrot.

It was a shockingly easy capture. Fat Thom dispatched

the parrot immediately to England as a wedding present for Princess Elizabeth, daughter of James I, who was about to marry Frederick, Elector Palatine of the Rhine in London.

This was the wedding at whose celebrations Shakespeare's *The Tempest* was first performed. Having survived a rough journey and upset by the climate, to his horror, the parrot was forced to sit on a lady-in-waiting's shoulder and watch one of the worst productions of *The Tempest* the world has ever seen. The parrot's genetic construction, however much he willed it to the contrary, ensured that every word sank ineradicably into his memory. Sensibly, he refrained from ever repeating any of it – including the *sotto voce* 'Oh no' from the bard himself, as Ariel slipped on a piece of orange peel and skidded across the apron stage into the wedding party. How the scions of literature would have torn that bird wing from wing had they known that Shakespeare's own voice was faithfully transcribed on his inch-long brain. He kept his counsel and tried to look dumb.

The parrot naturally developed a phobia about *The Tempest*. Why he should also have developed an irrational loathing of the philosopher and mathematician, René Descartes, is something I shall address later.

It was the parrot's destiny to find himself in Prague in 1619 at the momentous time when science started to split from magic. How did he get there?

After watching that odious version of *The Tempest*, the parrot underwent a severe attack of the shits and members of the Royal Household preferred not to have him sitting on their shoulder. In disgrace, he made the journey in his cage when the Electress Palatine left England for Heidelberg. It was the 28th of April, 1613. The ship was bound for Flushing. A northerly breeze ruffled the bird's feathers. The cold made him miserable.

He looked out bleakly over the cold, choppy waters as the royal party was brought to shore in a barge decked with crimson velvet. Twenty rowers kept in time to a band of musicians rowing in the stern. The parrot sulked. He was, however, cheered up by the rapturous welcome of the Dutch citizens whose applause and roars of approval he faithfully recorded and repeated out loud to himself on those occasions when his morale needed a boost, as it often did on this unasked for, cold-arsed tour of Europe. From Flushing, the party went to Rotterdam, then on to Delft and eventually Heidelberg.

Heidelberg suited the parrot. The castle was at the top of a steep ascent from the River Neckar. He besported himself in the formal gardens of the castle among magical curiosities such as the statue of Memnon, which emitted sounds when the sun's rays struck it, and he recorded the pneumatically controlled speaking statues. He was carried around on the shoulder of Inigo Jones during the latter's visit to the gardens and grottoes which were talked of as the eighth wonder of the world. Occasionally, he dipped his green tail feathers in the singing fountains. He listened half-heartedly to the debates of the Rosicrucians, Brotherhood of the Invisibles; yawned behind his wing at the arguments on Utopias and religious factionalism and disappeared into an ornamental box hedge whenever a troupe of actors arrived – even when it was known in advance that they were to perform an alchemical romance such as *The Chemical Wedding of Christian Rosencreutz* and had no intention of doing *The Tempest*.

It was at Heidelberg that the parrot first came in contact with Christianity. He was naturally sceptical. Hearing the story of the Annunciation, he was astounded by the ignorance of his human captors in not realising that the news had clearly been brought to Mary by a Great Parrot. When he compared what he heard about angels with what he knew about parrots, it was resoundingly obvious to him that parrots were the superior species. What does an angel have that a parrot doesn't? Multi-coloured wings? Forget it. Ability to speak in tongues? No bid. Have you ever seen an angel hold a great big mango in its claw and nibble at it? No. They sit there with their wings folded and an expression on their face like they just shit in their pants or something. The parrot preferred his own kind any day. Parrots fight and squabble and sulk and drop bits of food on the floor like normal people. Parrots live in the real world. They get drunk on the fumes from rotten fruit and fermented corn. Bravo and brilliante for us, cried the bird.

And so, at the University of Heidelberg, where strange and exciting influences, both mechanical and magical, developed rapidly during the reign of Elizabeth and Frederick, the parrot passed a time of such intellectual stimulus that he rarely gave a thought to the quarrelling rapids, surging rivers and thorny bushes of his own South American continent.

Despite a happy and settled life in Heidelberg, the October of 1619 found Monsignor Parrot (he had adopted a continental handle) in a covered cage, travelling clandestinely to Prague. When the cover was whipped off, he discovered that he had been the only one of the Royal Household travelling clandestinely and that everyone else was bowing and waving out of the carriage windows to the crowd, as the procession of magnificently embossed coaches swung giddily over the Vtlava Bridge, along the cobbled path and through the stone-jawed entrance to Prague Castle.

The Protestant Elector and Electress Palatine, whose wedding gift he was, had become the Winter King and Queen of Bohemia – a name coined by the Jesuits who said, quite accurately, that the couple would vanish with the winter snows, which, after the Catholic Hapsburgs attacked in the Battle of the White Mountain, they did.

However, before the Hapsburg attack, the wondrous city of Prague was host to every sort of cabbalist, alchemist and astronomer and housed the most up-to-date artistic and scientific collections. The parrot inspected the paintings of Arcimboldo the Marvellous (who had also been the Master of Masquerade) which showed men made of vegetables, tin pots and books. Tycho Brahe had discovered the fixed position of seven hundred stars and Johann Kepler raced to discover the periodic laws of planets. The Castle of Prague, through which the parrot fluttered nonchalantly, accustoming himself to his new habitat, contained Rudolfo's Room of Wonders and the wooden floor of the Great Hall thrummed with men walking up and down, arguing and debating. The room was lined with books, maps, globes and charts. Men discussed sea routes, navigational passages and astronomy. Ideas were propounded which made men's mouths dry with excitement and fear, giving them palpitations and erections, often at the same time.

However, the servants in the great gloomy castle inexplicably took against the exotic pets that had arrived with Elizabeth of Bohemia, whose foreign dress they regarded with suspicion. A monkey frightened a waiting-man by leaping on his shoulder. Food was deliberately tipped off the plate before it could be served. A serving girl threw cake at the parrot.

It all ended in a terrible scream.

When exactly, at what precise moment, did the parrot scream? Historians have battled for doctorates over both the cause and the timing of the scream, which was only the second time that the parrot had found it necessary to utter such a cry of warning. There has been as much scholastic dispute generated by that shriek as there has over the snort of the Nilus camel.

Some scholars say this:

Whilst unpacking the royal baggage, a serving-girl looked round for a place to put the crystal ship that was the christening gift from Prince Maurice of Orange to the firstborn son of Elizabeth and Frederick of Bohemia, the infant Prince Henry. The parrot cast one eye on the glittering boat and let out a prophetic scream that reverberated through the castle foretelling the dreadful end that was to befall the young prince.

What was this dreadful event? Well, years later, in exile in The Hague, the young Prince Henry and Frederick his father rode one winter's day to the Zuider Zee to see two ships from the Caribbean brought there by Dutch pirates. They wanted to see the booty. All the way there, the horses slipped and slid sideways along the icy roads.

It was dark when they arrived in the evening. Freezing mists caused chaos as oarsmen in soaking woollen mittens tried to outmanoeuvre each other to find the best position for boarding the galleons which towered overhead. There were shouts and oaths and the unstable light of lanterns through fog. Two small boats crashed in the dark. It was not until morning, in a grey lake bobbing with frozen horses' heads, that they found the corpse of young Prince Henry. The galleon was covered in ice, his body was entangled in the rigging. His collar and ruff lay stiffly under layers of hoar frost and his cheek, frozen to the mast, seemed in its icy transparency to have turned to crystal.

A life is always slung between two images, not two dates. Find the right image and you can foretell the manner of death. They say that the parrot foresaw the death as soon as he clapped eyes on the crystal ship, the sight of which caused him to shriek.

Not a bit of it.

Parrots are not well known for their prophetic abilities. They live for hundreds of years and are the owners of exceedingly good memories, but they cannot think forward for more than two ticks.

The next theory of the scream.

As is always the case in times of upheaval, a troupe of actors was wandering around Prague, looking for digs. The company was led by one Robert Browne. They had turned up to spend the winter in Prague after a long European tour which included moderately successful performances at the Frankfurt Fair and Heidelberg. The actors mooched around town looking for the best eating-houses and arguing over whether it was better to stick to their production of *The Tempest* or to introduce into the repertoire *The History of Susanna*, and, of course, fighting over who was to play what in which.

Could it have been a certain conversation, overheard by the bird, that caused its cry of distress?

Just before supper in the Lesser Hall, the parrot was seated on the stone sill of one of the slit windows. Beneath him, Robert Browne, manager of the troupe, was listening to an actor who thought he should be playing the part of Trinculo in *The Tempest*:

'Robert. I've had the most wonderful idea for Trinculo. If you will let me play the part, I thought it would be a good idea for Trinculo to make his first entrance with a parrot on his head.'

'I think not, Arthur. I don't want anything to distract from the text at that point.'

'It would be very realistic. We could borrow the parrot that belongs to the Queen's household.'

'The theatre is supposed to be a garden of illusion. Anything real would be a distraction.'

'It would get a laugh.'

'I'll think about it.'

Did the parrot emit his famous scream at this point? Not at all.

Rather, he emitted a disgusted groan that he had picked up from a crowd disappointed at the last-minute cancellation of a public execution. He managed to fly, notwithstanding, to the safety of the rafters, lest his greatest fear be realised and he be put in their production of *The Tempest*.

Just at this point, history intervened and saved him from one torment only to present him with another.

Unbeknownst to the Winter King and Queen or any of their household, on the cold night of November 10th, 1619, warmed by a German stove in a small house on the banks of the Danube, a young man slept and dreamed that mathematics was the sole key to the understanding of nature.

THE PARROT AND DESCARTES

His name was René Descartes. He spent all – or almost all – that winter meditating on this notion. Then came the news that the Duke of Bavaria and his Catholic army were about to march on the Winter King and Queen of Bohemia. Curiosity caused René Descartes, educated by Jesuits, to re-join his old regiment in order to see a little action.

And so it came about that Descartes, innocent symbol of reason, skulking in the back rows of the soldiery, watched and participated as little as possible as the Battle of the White Mountain was fought outside Prague. The battle put to flight the newly ensconced King and Queen, smashed the spirit of Bohemia and destroyed the unity of magic and science which had developed as one under the liberal auspices of Rudolfo and his successors. Magic and technology were, from then on, to go their separate ways.

Elizabeth and Frederick piled what they could into two carriages: children, a few staff, monkeys, the crystal christening gift and other sundry valuables. In the whirlwind rush to leave, they left behind, by accident, the Order of the Garter and the parrot.

Meanwhile, among the sweaty sergeants, bone-aching mercenaries and big-chinned Hapsburgs, marched one mathematically inclined soldier with a forgettable face, thoughtfully chewing on a piece of dried beef. The raggle-taggle, victorious army hobbled up the steep road leading to the castle walls. At the same time, a servant of the fleeing royals, who had been sent back to retrieve the Order of the Garter, but unable to find it, had grabbed the parrot in lieu, came running down through the ranks of the ascending army, holding the parrot aloft like a green-and-gold banner.

And so, for a brief moment, they came face to face. The master of rationalism and the parrot.

The parrot screamed and it was indeed the same disturbing and terrifying sound that had rent the air in the Orinoco basin when the earth split and a hand poked out and a white figure ran into the forest. The sound reverberated for days along the banks of the Vtlava, making the citizens of Prague shake their heads and wiggle their fingers around in their ears.

And it was thus that the man whose hidden presence in the conquering army might well have been their secret weapon, the man who contributed to the rout of a certain sort of imagination, the man who later claimed that common sense was the prime mover of men, the man who thought he was there because he was, or who was there because he thought he was, wandered into Prague in search of nothing more profound than a pork sausage on rye with mustard.

Thus was reason born, by chance, out of the dark disorder of war. The parrot had intuitively recognised the danger of a man who believed that animals were automatons and that parrots ceased to exist when they were asleep. But reason tells us reason has its limits, thought the parrot. And he was so delighted with his own wit, that he let out an involuntary laugh which had the servants searching all night for an intruder.

The parrot, ruffled by his moves around Europe, finally settled into unhappy exile with the rest of Elizabeth and Frederick's household in an apartment in The Hague which belonged to Prince Henry of Nassau. Later, the exiled family moved into a draughty and gloomy palace on the river near Leiden.

The Dutch phase of the parrot's life proceeded uneventfully

until the day in 1640 when, out of the blue, there was a loud knocking on the palace doors. Who should be standing on the doorstep, but René Descartes. Fortunately, the parrot's cage was covered and he slept with his beak tucked under his wing, unaware that his greatest nightmare (not including *The Tempest*) had sidled into the palace to discuss mathematics with the young princesses. When he awoke to see the unwelcome visitor he gave a dismal squawk. Nobody heeded his warning, although from around then mind and matter started to divide, body and soul to separate and science and magic to march in opposite directions.

The princesses of the household were shabby, handsome and gifted. The eldest, Princess Elizabeth, studied Cartesian philosophy until her nose went red. Descartes himself said that he had never met anyone who had such a grasp of his writings. However, soon she fell in love and had an affair with one of her ladies-in-waiting and Descartes sought solace (and financial reward) at the court of Queen Christina of Sweden. Despite himself, the parrot had picked up the rudiments of analytic geometry. He secretly took emetics to rid himself of the affliction. On foggy nights, before his cage was covered, he asked himself where rationalism had come from.

During this time the bird was lost in thought. What he thought about was the written word. Books had become the truth. The written word had become proof. Laws were built on books which contained precedent. People were killed in their name. Confession, word of mouth, rumour, gossip, chattiness and oratory had all lost their place in the hierarchy of power. Passports verified. Documents condemned. Signatures empowered. Books were the storage place of memory. Books were written to contradict other books.

The parrot, a natural representative of the oral tradition, began to sob. He used the sob he had heard in Lisbon of a young girl whose lover had been drowned at sea. He was fed up with the cobbled streets and castles, grey, snowy skies and the written word. He began to long for the chattering waters of the Essequibo River, the hot humid smells of the bush and the celestial choirs of humming howler monkeys. As solace, he often reproduced for himself the deep silence of the forests before words swarmed over the earth like cushi ants, the piccolo fluting call of a certain bird and the rushing of a thousand rivers over the rocks. He was unspeakably homesick.

And so when two of the sons of Frederick and Elizabeth, named Rupert and Maurice, discussed venturing to the Caribbean to seek elephants and rose-emeralds, the parrot, who was now allowed the freedom of the palace, decided to stow away.

In 1649, *The Antelope* was rigged up in the port of Rotterdam. Two years later the ship set sail with the parrot hiding in the cook's cabin where he dined to the sound of rushing waters and creaking timbers. Near the Virgin Islands, a squalling hurricane upturned the ship. Rupert landed but Maurice disappeared. As soon as the parrot felt the familiar, warm uplift of air over the Orinoco he relaxed on the wind and allowed the sun-heated breezes to carry him east. He found his way to a region, now known as Berbice, and for a long time, kept his head down in a mango tree, trying to make sense of his experiences.

The parrot had brought back with him:

a) Shakespeare's voice.

b) The tumultuous roar of a Dutch crowd on April 28th, 1613.

c) The sound of René Descartes scraping his plate with his spoon.

d) The scratch of Rembrandt's etching needle.

e) The heartrending sob of the Portuguese girl whose lover had drowned.

None of it was any use except the sob.

It was 1652. The parrot was almost dozing off when he heard two men conversing beneath where he sat in a tree. The speaker was one Père de la Borde, a Jesuit priest. He was talking to a Dutch merchant.

'The Indians are dreamy and melancholy. They sit silent for whole days at a time. They don't care about the past or the future. They get angry when I try to explain to them about Paradise because they do not want to have to die before they go there. I can't seem to persuade them to leave their present goods for future ones. They know nothing about either ambition or anxiety. What can I do? They are lazy, inconstant and wayward.'

He was addressing his remarks to Abraham van Peere, a tall Dutchman with an emaciated face, wrinkled hands and a spattering of freckles, who cursed the muddy banks on which they stood. Mould exploded in spectra of colour on his leather uppers. Rottenness ambushed his nose. He had arrived from Holland to build a life as a merchant. The priest continued.

'I shall probably be accompanying Père Meland, another Jesuit brother, to Santa Fe de Bogota,' continued Père de la Borde. 'He is a fine man. He had correspondence with René Descartes, the philosopher mathematician who died in Sweden recently. Père Meland is going to introduce the ideas of Descartes in a series of lectures at the Jesuit College there. Descartes' work *Meditations* which he converted to scholastic form will be the main topic of his lectures.

Ah well, how were those two men to distinguish one more parrot scream amongst the thousands that reverberate through the Orinoco basin and the Amazonas.

Time passed. It was clear to the bird that ideas from Europe were gaining ground in his own territory. This realisation was reinforced when a chartered vessel from New York arrived in Georgetown. It was now the year 1800. The parrot watched suspiciously as a cargo of canvas palaces and painted forests, cardboard trees, crowns, daggers, sceptres and chains was unloaded. The strolling players had arrived from North America, having toured the islands first.

Intimations of predestination should have warned the parrot to steer clear. His appetite for fruit, however, overcame his trepidation. They fed him. The actors, a group of bearded German Jews who also played the female roles, began to rehearse as they chewed on mango seeds and cast them aside. On the first night of their concert party, a furious fight broke out between the 'female' singers and the orchestra. The bearded actresses hitched up their gowns over their hips, revealing filthy pantaloons, and began a regular boxing match. It was decided to dispense with the orchestra. They would do excerpts from *The Tempest*.

The parrot was snatched once more from a real tree and chained to a cardboard one. Every now and then he released his sob. As Prospero came forward to deliver his final epilogue, the bemused audiences heard two voices speaking at once:

> . . . now I want
> Spirits to enforce, art to enchant;
> And my ending is despair,
> Unless I be relieved by prayer,
> Which pierces so, that it assaults
> Mercy itself, and frees all faults.
> As you from crimes would pardon'd be,
> Let your indulgence set me free.

At the end of the tour in 1801, the parrot, wings clipped and wearing an ornamental chain on one leg, set off wearily for a new life in North America.

THE FABLE OF
THE TWO SILVER PENS

I am writing these words with a silver pen, or rather a silvery-looking pen. This year, on my birthday, my husband gave it to me as a present. In fact, it's probably stainless steel but a handsome pen all the same, both beautiful and business-like, made by a firm of pen-makers centuries old.

Usually I write on a personal computer but for a while I had suffered from writer's block, bogged down with notes and discarded ideas. Initially, I took up the pen to see if writing in longhand would help. Although the pen was supposed to be no more than an elegant symbol of my trade, I must say I enjoyed the physical act of writing once more and was pleased with the result. By using the pen I seemed to tap into some hitherto inaccessible source of energy and truth. For several days I wrote like a fiend. I found that, with incredible speed, I had completed a short story.

I entered the work for a literary competition. Soon after that the telephone rang and a pleasant voice informed me that I had won an award. I attended the ceremony. In addition to a substantial sum of money I was presented with a silver pen, or rather a silvery-looking pen. It was in all respects identical to the one given me by my husband. When I got home, I showed it to him and we laughed. It was indistinguishable from the one he had bought me.

Except that the second pen wrote lies.

It took me a while to discover this. Naturally, I assumed that it would make no difference whichever pen I used. But gradually I noticed that the prize pen wrote fluently and could always be relied on to produce something acceptable and polished but false. Whereas my gift pen either wrote feverishly and truthfully or it did not write at all. Once I had discovered this, I took care to keep the two pens apart, keeping the gift pen always about my person and the prize pen in its case in the bureau drawer.

When the gift pen started to write incoherently, as it did with increasing frequency, I was tempted to rely more on the ever plausible prize pen. I found myself hovering around the desk which contained the pen like someone who has given up smoking but knows that there is still a pack of cigarettes in the drawer. After an immense effort, I finally resolved to use only the pen which my husband had given me. Despite its writing in fits and starts, its tendency to scribble gibberish, its refusals to write at all, I knew that somewhere within itself it contained the real stuff of writing. Even in fictional terms, it wrote the truth. I have used it ever since.

The question is: With which pen am I writing this fable?

THE
SPARKLING
BITCH

It was precisely this sort of behaviour that made Charles Hay furious with his wife. He sat in the front seat next to the driver. His shirt, starched and clean that morning, had begun to wilt. They had pulled up at a small petrol station somewhere along the open dusty road from Ibadan to Lagos for her to use the lavatory. He waited impatiently. There was too much blank sky in this country for his liking. Too much heat and too much oppressive emptiness. He had been glad to leave behind the large tracts of land and the few devastated villages which his own company had left stinking of oil spillages. The mess offended him. Having ordered a cursory clean-up, necessitated by embarrassing but manageable international protest, his business was completed. Now he just wanted to return home to London. Usually his wife did not accompany him on these trips. She spent most of her time in England in their small Sussex cottage. There was no doubt that she was being deliberately perverse, as usual. He tried resting his elbow on the silvered frame of the open car window but the sun had made it too hot to bear.

'Susan, come on,' he called out through the car window towards the petrol pump. The hot air swallowed his words.

His watch said ten-past twelve. They had two and a half hours to reach Lagos Airport. Enough time, but all the same . . . he was a meticulous man.

Susan Hay, wearing a short-sleeved cotton blouse and tailored stone-coloured shorts, was crouched, motionless, beside the single petrol stand. Near her, leaning against the pump, was a boy of about thirteen. He was clearly the victim of starvation: his thin black limbs were crossed and sharply folded like those of a spider playing dead.

He had been hidden from sight by the petrol pump when she went in, but a glimpse of him startled her when she came back out from the toilets. She had not initially recognised that it was a person. The angularity of the black body outlined against the pale concrete forecourt and the faded red gasoline pump made her freeze with shock when she realised. Despite skeletal thinness, the boy's figure resonated with a sort of violent power. The sharp angles made by his arms and legs reminded her of a runic letter she had once seen carved in stone. Susan Hay squatted down and pulled a US fifty-dollar note from her purse. She offered it to him but he did not move, so she placed it in the bowl at his side and swivelled on her heels looking round for a stone or something to stop it blowing away in the warm gritty breeze. Not finding anything, she fished in her bag once more and put some coins on top of the dollar bill to anchor it down. Then, for some reason, she settled on her haunches and just stayed there in the heat next to the boy.

She had been squatting like that for about five minutes when her husband shouted out to her from the car. An irrational empathy kept her there. Her husband's voice sounded distant. Understanding that she needed some response from the figure at her side in order to be released from this spell, she frowned to herself without changing her posture. It was not gratitude that she needed exactly. She was not sure what it was. Perhaps just an acknowledgement of her existence.

'Are you all right?' she asked.

The boy turned his head towards her. The movement pulled the yellow-black skin so tightly over the cheekbones that she could see the cavernous hollow beneath and a faint mocking pulse of life in the neck. His mouth opened to release a fetid breath, but no sound came out from between lips cracked like parched mud-flats. A few misshapen teeth stuck out at odd angles. His eyelids had been bitten by insects but the eyes beneath were huge and dark and compelling. He said nothing but an exchange had taken place. The brief contact enabled her to break free. She said goodbye and clambered back into the scorching interior of the car.

Five minutes on down the road they were involved in a hold-up. The thrusting black muzzle of the gunman's pistol penetrated the driver's window. First of all he had danced in the road in front of them waving them down. When the driver tried to swerve round him, he fired a shot which hit a billboard advertising Shell petrol at the side of the road. He wore ill-fitting military brown, green and yellow camouflage trousers and T-shirt, like a badly painted stage set. Adrenalin empowered the jitterbugging aggressor with energy as he looked through the window at the occupants of the car.

'I want your money. Give me your money now.' His eyes were popping from their sockets. Globules of sweat flew off his forehead as he glanced up and down the road for other vehicles, gesticulating wildly with the gun. The driver stared straight ahead, terrified.

'These people do not have money,' muttered the driver weakly, doing his best to protect his passengers. The gunman re-materialised miraculously on Charles Hay's side of the car and spotted the Rolex watch on his victim's wrist.

'Give me that watch. You are telling lies,' he protested furiously to the driver. 'How do you think Nigeria is ever going to get ahead as a country if people like you tell lies. We will never get anywhere.' He seemed genuinely outraged as he pocketed the watch. He took and stuffed in his trouser pocket the handful of banknotes which Susan Hay was proffering from the back. Still glaring at the driver, he slammed his open hand down on the roof of the car. The thunderous noise inside the car made them all jump. He backed off waving the car on like an official. When they dared to look back he was jumping over the dried-grass bank at the roadside. It was all over in less than two minutes.

Charles Hay felt relieved to be in the City of London again. After their return from Nigeria he decided to take some exercise by walking to work early in the morning. The streets were still deserted. The route from his Barbican flat took him past the Lloyd's building. Although he was sixty-seven years old, he approved of the new Lloyd's building which wore its glass and tubular-steel intestines on the outside. As he looked up, the transparent bubble of the lift, also on the outside, was descending down the side of the building, giving the impression that the occupant, a man in a dark suit with his head bent forward, was being slowly hanged.

It occurred to Hay, mischievously, that the more transparent the new buildings in the City of London looked, the shadier the dealings that went on inside. An inverse ratio of glass, light and windows to dark dealings. Or rather sharp dealings. Dealings that moved with such speed as to be invisible and lethal. Bomb-damage dealings. He kicked away some fragments of glass from underfoot to the sound of tinkling arpeggios – shards that had been hurled to the street in a recent bomb attack on the City.

When he had started work in the City as a young man, the place had mostly consisted of sombre granite edifices containing offices with panels of opaque glass in the doors as if they were all occupied by private detective agencies. Creaky old lifts with folding latticed iron doors connected the floors. Now a series of increasingly flirtatious buildings had arisen amongst those ponderous and impenetrable blocks of stone: delicate angular structures of dark glass reflecting bronze sky and clouds, from which you could no more guess what went on inside than you could guess what a blind man was thinking from the reflection in his glasses. Other new buildings that had sprung up made him feel as though he were walking through kids' puzzles grown large. Lego sets. Everything had become a game. Business had become fun – as he had always felt it should be. At last he felt in tune with the times.

Despite his age, the modern architecture suited him. There was something insubstantial about the new buildings that matched his own swift and lightly conducted business manoeuvres. Contracts in Nigeria were fulfilled and over-night the company moved on to explore the possibilities in Colombia. The architecture somehow reflected this new phantasmagoria of commerce. Now you see it, now you don't. A fly-by-night affair; houses of glass cards thrown up overnight by sleight of hand, full of sharp angles and sharp practice. Tomorrow they might disappear and be replaced by another set of transparent hexagons, pyramids and domes. After all, he pondered as he continued his brisk walk to work, everything was fragmenting these days: the Soviet bloc, the old monolithic ideas, grand notions of a fairer world, all these were disintegrating. It was important to keep up with what was going on. Nowadays it was as if the City of London had changed sex. Having once been a solid and patriarchal affair of granite and stone with all the solemn weight of imperialism, it had now become a sparkling bitch in glass petticoats with see-through flighty underwear. An alluring transvestite city, light-headed and capricious but concealing dangerous muscle. After centuries, the feminine partner in the business tango had finally decided to reveal herself.

Charles Hay was head of Hay Oil Incorporated. He lived and breathed the new rarefied atmosphere of the City. He was always in his office immaculately dressed by seven o'clock in the morning, sitting behind his desk in a faint haze of after-shave. Manicured hands in double-cuffed shirts with monogrammed gold cuff-links flicked through the day's business papers. The fey tilt of his head when he listened to the reports of his senior executives gave no indication that he could move, in transactions, with the speed and unpredictability of a funnel spider. He cared about appearances. More than anything else, he cared about appearances. That also stamped him as one of the modernists in his field. He understood the primacy of image.

The public image of his company beamed out regularly in television advertisements which consisted of a slow camera pan round magnificent white Palladian buildings to the accompaniment of a Bach cantata and ending with the words 'Hay Oil' in classically simple script across the screen. If there was something slightly fake about the advertisements, the impression that the perfect marble pillars and white cornices were a façade, a film set rather than the real thing, it was intentional. The Parthenon in Athens had been suggested as a location for the advertisement but the original turned out to be too chipped and grubby for Charles Hay's taste.

The offices themselves, another gigantic concoction of glass, were in Lombard Street. Everything inside the entrance lobby was elegantly faked. Marble-clad floors. Artificial streams and waterfalls. Mock palm trees festooned with lianas. Stuffed parrots. Tapes of tropical birdsong. The air too was fake, warm and humid on a bright cold spring day. There were fake smiles on the lips of secretaries as their metronome heels clicked over the marble floors on their way to the lifts.

The private life of Charles Hay was kept well away from public gaze. Having stayed a bachelor for most of his life, he had married Susan late when she was twenty-three and he was forty-five. Now, twenty-two years later, her appearance was still slender and girlish. The bone structure of her face remained as striking as it had been in her modelling days. Her reddish nut-brown hair hung straight in a schoolgirl cut. There had been, until recently, a sense of mischief in her brown eyes.

Susan Hay, her husband discovered soon after their marriage, was intelligent as well as perverse. In the first flush of his infatuation, he had taken pleasure in watching her argue spiritedly at dinner parties. She had the habit of playing devil's advocate, always taking the unexpected side in a dispute. He rather admired this coquettish defiance, the lack of concern for convention. It amused him. That was at first. Later, he found that she could be infuriatingly stubborn. Once she turned up at his office on a bicycle wearing an old mackintosh. He was irritated by such behaviour. Her eccentricities began to exasperate him. He bought her a cottage in the country and they fell into the habit of a discreet estrangement although this had never been fully discussed.

Neither of them wanted a divorce. Susan no longer really knew how to earn her own living. It suited her better to remain in the country and read or scribble her own poetry and go for long walks. People were surprised that she still mentioned with pride the fact that she had gained four O levels as if it were a recent achievement. Sometimes she strummed a few chords on a guitar over and over again, having made no progress after the first few lessons. Her abilities, for some reason, never developed. There was something bleak and austere about the cottage. She kept the grey floorboards bare apart from a few hippy cushions and an old settee. There was no sign of the wealth to which she had access.

Charles never contemplated divorce. That would have been contrary to his public image of perfection. When it was necessary, Susan was happy to appear at his side looking stunning, although he always felt a little wary in her company. She sometimes contradicted him in public with an air of childish defiance which he no longer found charming. Once, at dinner, he had laughed politely at someone's joke and she had embarrassed him by asking out loud, 'Was that laugh genuine or was it false?'

But many people congratulated him on his beautiful and

wayward wife. She undoubtedly possessed talents that would reveal themselves in time. Hers were the qualities of a deer, fleet, delicate and elusive. It pleased him to realise that other people still found her captivating.

In the offices of Hay Oil, fastidious standards were maintained. One section of the public relations team was employed solely to keep an eye on the appearance and demeanour of the workforce. All instances of slovenliness were reported to Charles Hay personally. Anyone with a marginally unclean collar, bitten fingernails, scuffed shoes, dandruff or any other hint of lack of personal hygiene was liable to be hauled up in front of him. His office was known as the 'incinerator' because of the scorching interviews that took place with offenders.

Shares in the company prospered. Minor protests about company policy abroad were always met with swift denials and an enormous public relations offensive to deflect criticism and disseminate images of an environmentally responsible and concerned parent company.

Hay, still sprightly for his age, ran up the flight of steps in front of his office building. By the time the morning mail arrived he had already done an hour's work. His devoted middle-aged secretary came in triumphantly waving the invitation that he had been hoping for all year. The invitation was for Mr and Mrs Charles Hay to attend the Guildhall banquet at which the Chancellor of the Exchequer made his annual speech. As he studied the invitation a glow of satisfaction radiated through him. It asked Mr and Mrs Hay to join the Chancellor at the high table. This year was the first time that he had ever been invited to sit on the high table with the Chancellor. It meant that under the television lights he would be publicly visible, sitting alongside the new Mayor of London, the Governor of the Bank of England and other City luminaries. It was the supreme accolade for a businessman, an acknowledgement that his business practice was appreciated by the New Labour Party now in power, a party with which he felt considerable affinity. It was an honour which he had craved for years.

Nine months had passed since their return from Nigeria. On consulting his diary, Charles Hay was surprised to realise that he had not seen Susan once during that time although they had spoken often on the phone. In fact, it was not unusual for long periods to pass without their meeting. Both of them were quite content to let matters drift on this way. Since their return, he had tried more than once to arrange an amicable meal together. She would agree to come up to town and then, a day or so later, he would find a message on his answerphone saying, 'Can we have a rain-check on the meal, sweetie? I've got a bit of a cold.' Or some other excuse.

He telephoned Susan to give her the date of the banquet and ensure that she would be present at his side.

'Of course, darling. Wild horses wouldn't stop me being there. It's wonderful. I can't wait.'

'Wear the green Versace dress that I like, Susan.'

'OK.' She laughed. 'If you want, darling.'

Recently one or two of Susan Hay's neighbours in Sussex had tried to get hold of Charles Hay because they were worried about her. They thought she did not look well. But when he called she insisted that she was fine and joked about how nosy neighbours were in the country. She had been seen walking alone on the Sussex downs, always wearing the same dirty old mackintosh. She was thin and walked with her head cast slightly to one side. What the neighbours did not know was that, on one occasion when she had walked all the way to Lewes and sat, exhausted, without moving, on a bench for hours, the local police had questioned her, mistakenly thinking that she was a vagrant. She had thought it was hugely funny.

Sometimes, in the cottage, Susan stayed for hours in a rocking-chair covered with a shawl. The remains of brown rice meals stayed on the table for days. At other times, she sat on the floor and arranged her body in the same foetal position as the boy she had seen in Nigeria, staying cramped up like that all afternoon, without eating or moving, through dusk and until after nightfall. She did not understand why she did it, but it satisfied her in some way.

As a child, Susan had been put for a few months into an orphanage when her mother suffered a nervous breakdown. Whether or not this was the cause of her interior self becoming barren, a wasteland, nobody knew. When people spotted her walking on the downs, she seemed to carry the aura of the orphanage with her, as though she were part of a parade of orphans, thousands of them, invisible, walking in pairs around the grounds of their institutions, hand in comfortless hand. Acquaintances hesitated before approaching her and then turned away pretending they had not seen her. She would either ignore them or make some painful attempt at conversation.

Her reclusiveness intensified. Despite what everyone had recognised early on as her undoubted potential, these barren areas where nothing reached fruition, these patches of wasteland, of arrested development, still existed inside her. After their return from Nigeria, in the spaces where those budding gifts might have grown, a strange and powerful god gradually emerged to stalk the clearings; a god so extraordinary and so attractive that she became bound to him and mastered by him. He began to rule her with a rod of iron until there was no distinguishing between her and himself. She welcomed this implacable god of starvation, who opposed all fertility, excess and fecundity, as her deliverance and abandoned herself to a ruler of the utmost severity.

'Charles.'

'Patrick.'

Conversation hummed amongst the guests in evening dress under the vaulted dark wooden beams of the Guildhall. The Lord Lieutenant of Essex, hooked nose, red cheeks, grasped Charles Hay's shoulder and shook him by the hand before continuing to push his way, beaming, through the people milling around outside the great banqueting hall.

'Better find out where we're sitting,' the Lord Lieutenant called back over his shoulder. He winked and nodded towards his wife as he went to consult the list of placements.

Through the swing doors, uniformed employees of the catering company were visible inside the banqueting hall, moving quietly to and fro, putting the final touches to the décor. Bowls of roses entwined with glossy laurel leaves decked each table. Every crystal wine goblet and every solid silver fork was checked. Television crews climbed to the best vantage points for filming, ensuring that the three great crystal chandeliers would not interfere with camera sight-lines.

In the lobby, the familiar faces of political commentators and financial analysts showed themselves, mingling with people, ready to interpret at the drop of a hat the implications of the Chancellor's speech for the nation.

The Chancellor himself mixed freely with the guests, aware that eyes were upon him. He threw his head back and laughed at someone's joke, the wavy black hair worn swept back and his dark-brown eyes somehow giving the impression of an Italian opera diva confidently about to sing her most famous aria. He caught Charles Hay's eye for a second in a glance of affable recognition as he bent his ear to listen to his partner in conversation.

Enjoying the effects of this brief but precious moment of communication with the Chancellor, the exquisitely groomed Charles Hay elbowed his way politely to the street entrance to check on Susan's arrival. He had sent the chauffeur with the car down to Sussex to ensure that she would be on time. The evening air closed in on him, chilly and dank, as he stepped outside into the relative dark of the street. Brightly lit cars and taxis pulled up in turn. There was no sign of Susan. A twinge of annoyance hardened the lines around his mouth as he went back inside.

Dinner was announced. Guests were invited to take their places. With a growing sense of disbelief, Charles Hay made his way to the high table and sat down next to his wife's empty place. Within minutes, the dinner was under way. First there was the loyal toast to the Queen and then waiters and waitresses in their black-and-white uniform scurried about making sure that glasses were filled again for the toast to the Chancellor. Charles Hay, humiliated by the empty space next to him, tried to look relaxed as he sipped occasional spoonfuls of pink crab soup.

The Chancellor rose to speak. The hall fell quiet in a hush of anticipation. All attention focused on the attractive sensuous features of the minister. In the body of the hall, heavy linen napkins dabbed at mouths and were laid aside, glasses were put down and evening dresses rustled as guests leaned back to listen. The Chancellor ran his hand through his thick black hair with practised diffidence before embarking on his speech. Apart from his voice on the microphone, the only sound came from whirring cameras and the tinkling of a glass here or there.

No one saw Susan Hay enter the hall. Everybody was facing away from her towards the raised table. She did not weigh more than six stone and could barely walk. The green dress that Charles had suggested she wore hung off her like the last winter leaves on a skeletal tree. Her dark-red hair fell to her shoulders in dull greasy clumps. Untended for the past year, thick brown toenails sprouted from the ends of her feet. She had not been able to fasten the straps of her open-toed shoes properly because her ankles were too swollen. She clutched her invitation and looked around for Charles, a rictus smile on her lips.

As she moved like a murderous ghost between tables littered with crumbs and half-full wine glasses, people, sensing that something was terribly wrong, gradually turned round to look. Guests shifted their chairs enabling her to pass. Some people recoiled in shock as she approached like some living accusation. An iron will had her in thrall. She moved one leg after the other as if she were fitted with false limbs.

At one time, Susan Hay would have hated arriving late at

a formal banquet. Now it did not seem to trouble her in the least. She recognised Mrs Robert Seifert, dressed in a whirl of dark crimson shot-silk, her round face puckered with concern, and managed to nod in her direction, although most of her concentration was taken up with the act of walking. At last she seemed to have found her vocation, committing herself irrevocably to The Great Refusal with a ferocity and determination that no one suspected she possessed. She was fascinated by the directness and honesty of it. Who would have guessed that the answer to everything could be so simple? Do not eat. The god she honoured reciprocated by turning her into a blazing witness.

Charles Hay watched his wife, transfixed. He could not believe that this creature, who was clearly dying, would attempt to come and sit next to him. He burned with rage. A rippling murmur went through the hall. The Chancellor, disconcerted, looked up from his notes. Alerted by his momentary hesitation, some of the cameramen followed his gaze and then turned their cameras on Susan Hay.

Charles Hay had gone pale. He stayed still like a traitor, betraying his wife by refusing to stand and show her where he was. It was Robert Seifert who rose and took Susan by the arm – an arm that was almost pure bone. Gently he guided her towards her place. Dinner guests tried not to look as she passed. Charles' eyes remained fixed on the Chancellor.

'Sorry I'm late, poppet,' she managed to whisper as Robert Seifert helped her into her seat.

Charles remained turned rigidly away from her but he could smell her foul breath. He did not turn away completely because he was being televised. After what felt to him like an age, a round of applause signified the end of the Chancellor's speech.

After two other speakers had risen to thank the Chancellor and make their own brief contributions to the evening, the room relaxed into a buzz of conversation. Waitresses moved about with coffee and brandies.

A dreadful smell permeated the part of the room where Charles Hay and his wife sat. At last Charles managed to recover enough breath to speak.

'We're leaving,' he hissed. 'I'm taking you straight to a hospital.'

When Susan rose shakily to her feet, uncontrollable diarrhoea had stained her dress and dripped from the chair.

White with fury, Charles Hay took her by the arm and led her slowly from the hall.

ERZULIE

'I want to get out of here,' mumbled Mrs Rita Jenkins, previously Miss Rita Rimpersaud, as she lumbered like a tank from the bathroom into the living-room. Her husband stood reading his newspaper against the light from the window. There were tears in her eyes as she repeated the information with a hiccuping sob.

'I want to leave.'

She had just lowered herself on to the toilet only to have her broad behind greeted by a flight of frogs from the toilet bowl.

Armand Jenkins lowered the paper and looked at her with the expression of helpless exasperation that he kept in store for such occasions. He blinked at her several times to indicate blameless bewilderment. His wife was the only person who could induce in him this mien of defencelessness, of not knowing quite what to do. He rather enjoyed it. It made him feel like a little boy again. At work, there was no room for any such hints of vulnerability or indecision.

'But, honey, you said you wanted to come – that you were longing to see the old place again,' he almost pleaded.

Rita Jenkins sat on the taut surface of a sofa expensively

135

covered in pink-and-mauve chintz. It just managed to resist her weight, indenting slightly. There were three of these giant sofas in the living-room with arms and cushions shaped like stone boulders. The imposing sofas formed three sides of a square which contained a glass coffee table.

'I did,' she whined, 'but frogs just jumped out of the toilet. I forgot about frogs.' She wrinkled her brown nose in distaste. Her shoulders lifted and dropped again. 'And I miss Sally.' Their daughter had remained behind in Canada to study garden landscaping. She pursed her lips and tried to look pathetic – difficult in one whose solid expanse of chest formed such an unassailable frontispiece.

When Rita's husband had been posted to Guyana to supervise the operations of Omai Gold Mining Ltd, an offshoot of Canadian parent companies, Cambior and Golden Star Resources, she had been delighted at the thought of meeting old school chums again and catching up on their news. At the age of twenty-one she had migrated from Guyana to Canada with her family who were wealthy Guyanese jewellers. Two years later, she married an equally wealthy Canadian mining engineer, Armand Jenkins. Twenty years after that, when her husband's work required him to spend some time in Guyana, she jumped at the chance to return and show off a little in front of her less fortunate contemporaries.

On their return, the Jenkinses rented part of an enormous, gracious, old-style house in Main Street. The Canadian company paid for their living area to be refurbished throughout. As the house boasted some twenty rooms, far too many for the two of them, they only used the second floor. The rest of the house remained a dusty monument to the days of its past glory, full of ancient dressers, old local paintings, curios and knick-knacks, including an Amerindian skull the top of which had been carved as a lid for use as a vanity box. There was even a four-poster bed in one room. Rita could be heard schlep-schlepping heavily along the corridors in her half-slippers, checking for dust or disorder in her own quarters. The rest of the house she ignored.

'Either my nose is paranoid or this bathroom smells unhealthy,' she complained to the housekeeper, Adèle, as she sniffed around the place for bad odours. But, on the whole, Rita luxuriated as of old in the warmth of the climate and the free flow of breezes in the house after her severely air-conditioned abode in Canada. The staff, who arrived daily, outnumbered the occupants by five.

Back in Guyana once more, Rita Jenkins greeted past acquaintances with warmth, curiosity and the satisfaction which came with seeing how much more prosperous than them she had become. This state of affairs made her bountiful.

'Have it. Keep it. Go on, it's yours,' she would say, simpering, smiling and nodding encouragement as one of her friends looked longingly at a silk blouse hanging in the walk-in wardrobe or stroked the head of a small wooden sculpture. From the kitchen, the sound of the mixer whizzing up rum swizzles, in the way that Rita liked them with milk and a little essence of vanilla, signalled the arrival of elevenses. The drinks were usually served on a silver tray in the parlour by Margot, the solid deaf-mute servant employed on a casual basis by Adèle the housekeeper.

Now it was nine months after her arrival and Rita had had enough. Armand's contract was for two years. He spent long periods away at Omai, supervising the mining operations. She was bored. The novelty had worn off. She wanted to return to Canada. Apart from the constant electricity blackouts and water cuts, she had recently begun to receive a series of unsettling phone calls on their private and ex-directory number.

'Hello, I'm calling from Berbice.' The unknown woman's voice was high and obsequious.

'Who is this, please?' a puzzled Rita had enquired.

'Oh don' worry wid dat. I just want to talk to you. Is your husband there? You're so nice. How have you been today?'

'I think you must have the wrong number.'

'Is that the residence of Mr and Mrs Armand Jenkins?'

'Yes. This is our private number. If you wish to talk about official business please call the offices of Omai Gold Mining Ltd during office hours.'

'No. It's all right. I just wanted to have a little talk. How you doing?'

'What is it that you want?' Rita was becoming slightly unnerved. 'Is it a visa to Canada?' Armand Jenkins was known to have influence in obtaining those precious Canadian visas.

'Not really. I just wanted to know that everything is going through OK with you. Just a little "Hi and Bye" call. I'll check next week and see that things are going along fine. Goodbye.'

There had been several such calls from the woman Rita Jenkins referred to as 'the mad lady from Berbice'.

She sulked on the sofa. Armand had gone back to reading his newspaper. Rita shook off her sandals and planted her broad, bare feet on the floor. Bored and under-occupied, she reached for a chocolate from the blue ceramic dish on the coffee table, persuading herself that she must eat them in order to prevent them melting.

'And then there's that awful Shallow-Grave case,' grumbled Rita, shuddering as she put her feet up on the sofa and munched.

'I'm just reading about it,' said Armand, engrossed in the paper.

The woman was known as Shallow-Grave because that was the way she disposed of her victims, or alleged victims, along the banks of the Essequibo River.

The first body to be discovered was that of a sailor who disappeared from his Filipino ship while it was docked for repairs. The ship had been bringing, amongst other cargoes, some of the cyanide compounds necessary for the mining company at Omai. No one could guess how the unfortunate victim had made his last journey from Tiger Bay to the banks of the Essequibo near Supenaam. But one month later, the great tidal river nudged him back to the sandy surface of the river shore about half a mile from the village of Good Hope. Others followed.

Even in a country with a river for a backbone, where surprise offerings were frequently thrown up to the villagers who lived on its shores, no one was prepared for the assortment of corpses which the river put on display along its edge over the next few months: three fishermen, two foreign seamen and a surveyor who had been measuring the volumetric discharge and tidal flow of the waters. Shouts were raised on the stretch of river between the villages of Makeshift and Perseverance, usually by those doing a spot of night-fishing, as each new discovery was made. There had been eight corpses in all. Nobody knew the total count.

In Georgetown, where the case was being heard, people flocked to the courtroom to see for themselves the tall, stately woman accused of this string of murders. The public gallery groaned and heaved with men and women sweating, jostling, fanning themselves and jockeying for the best position to catch a glimpse of the woman who stood in the dock.

She remained elegant and dignified, somewhat aloof, with a cool demeanour that made many of the onlookers in the gallery appear to be more likely candidates for the charges made against her. People strained forward, not only to get a better look, but as if, by reaching closer, they might be able to dip into one of the blackwater creeks of the Essequibo region and escape the broiling heat. The air surrounding her seemed to be of a considerably lower temperature than the air in the rest of the courtroom. When Shallow-Grave leaned forward, the crowd leaned forward. When Shallow-Grave left the room at lunchtime, the atmosphere returned to one of habble and babble and clatter, everyday business and heat, the black radiance of a dark lake having moved elsewhere.

One woman in the public gallery never took her eyes from Shallow-Grave. It was Margot the sixty-year-old deaf mute who had not missed one day of the trial. Round her broad-domed head, which was slightly too large for her body, she tied the same faded triangular grey headscarf in a tight band so that no hair showed. Her large head made her powerful hands and arms seem disproportionately short and stubby. Her complexion was matt black with a porous quality like pumice stone, which never shone and seemed to absorb heat. Her mouth, pink and wet as a water-melon, always remained slightly open. She wore an old grey sweat-stained T-shirt and sat in the front row with her elbows on her knees and her chin resting on her fists, concentrating intently on the figure in the dock.

Before she found work with the Jenkins, Margot used to walk every day from Werk-en-Rust to Subryanville to wash and iron for a lawyer and his wife, both of whom did good works. They paid her too little and she left. She took in washing and ironing at home but a nagging pain in her right arm forced her to stop. Now she lived on a pittance made from the few hours of domestic work she could find. Three mornings a week, she helped out in the kitchen of the Jenkinses' rented house in Main Street.

The rest of the staff were curious about Margot, not least because she had mysteriously disappeared for a month recently and arrived back without a word of explanation. They also maintained a prurient interest in Margot's reaction to her Great Disappointment. Everyone knew that for years Margot had nursed an overpowering desire to migrate to Brooklyn. She shook and trembled when she thought of Brooklyn. Brooklyn was her Holy Grail. When she walked the streets of Georgetown, whether in stupefying heat or tropical downpour, her mind and hopes were pinned on Brooklyn. She was what is known as 'waiting to be sent for'. In other words, a friend of hers had already gone ahead to the United States and had written to Margot telling her that papers had been lodged applying for permission for Margot to join her. That was four years ago.

From that time on, Margot had received no news, either from the American Embassy or from her friend. Mr and Mrs Jenkins' housekeeper, Adèle, had once accompanied

Margot to the embassy in order to act as interpreter. The two women had inched their way along in a slow-moving line under the blazing sun. But it appeared that the papers had gone missing.

When they returned to the house, Margot resumed her duties with the other women in the kitchen, squeezing grapefruits and pouring the green juice into a glass jug. Adèle tentatively indicated that perhaps the papers had never been lodged in the first place. The outrage that this suggestion raised in Margot, the look of shocked betrayal on her face, prevented Adèle from ever mentioning it again. Margot had dropped the grapefruit and pounded her fists on the table in a passion.

'Ook-in. Ook-in.' Her thick lips opened wide and the others glimpsed a stub of pink tongue as she struggled to pronounce the word.

'Ook-in. Ook-in,' she continued in a shouting grunt. And then, amidst general laughter, the other women noticed that Margot's face was streaming with tears.

No one quite understood what was happening to Margot. She did not fully understand it herself. But what Adèle had said struck her with terror as she finally realised she was not going anywhere. With all her daydreams of a future in Brooklyn smashed, she had begun to wander around Georgetown and see, as if for the first time, the situation in which life had placed her.

She saw streets of tumbling, ramshackle houses, hutches and sheds, slum dwellings tacked together with criss-cross pieces of fencing, and she felt as though she herself had become as dry and sucked of moisture as the sun-bleached grey timbers. Her own headscarf too was grey with wear and sweat. When she chanced to catch sight of it, her large face looked grey, the colour of old lava. The greyness was all around her and everything inside her too seemed to have crumbled into grey dust. Her shoes had more or less disintegrated, peeling open like old, blackened banana skins in their unequal battle against unpaved roads, stones, rains, mud, sun and dust. Every alley had its own stench of frying food, of fly-infested garbage, stagnant pools and rotting planks. She felt like a ghost in her own city. A jumbie. Nobody seemed to notice her. She could have been invisible.

When she was arrested for trying to sell some cans of paint that turned out to have been stolen, she took no evasive action. She just raised her large head and looked up at the policeman with incomprehension, her mouth open, as if she were raking his face for an explanation not just of her arrest, but of her whole predicament. She had allowed herself to be taken quietly to the lock-up at La Penitence and sat, patient and defeated, through all the procedures that brought her finally to the women's jail in New Amsterdam to serve a month's sentence.

It was in the jail that she met Shallow-Grave.

Shallow-Grave occupied one of the three special cells reserved for notorious or first-degree criminals. On the few occasions when the other women came anywhere near her – for she had her own special escort – they noticed that Shallow-Grave was always clean and smelt good. There was something sparkling about her. And she sang beautifully, in her cell, with a voice that was sometimes low and husky but ranged upwards to a clear, rippling, thrilling soprano.

One day when Margot stood in the courtyard with four other inmates, Shallow-Grave was unlocked from her cell and appeared, escorted by a weary-looking, squat prison officer. She was being taken to empty her chamber-pot in one of the four stinking latrines at the top of a flight of wooden stairs to the right of the yard. Margot watched her as she mounted the rackety steps and pulled open the door of the cabin. When she emerged, she stood at the top of the steps, a statuesque figure, with the blue china chamber-pot glinting in the sun. Against the dried dead wood of the latrines, her skin shone a vibrant black. She wore a shoulderless, dark-blue cotton dress, slimline, with a white frill on the hem like the coastal waves of the Atlantic Ocean. As she surveyed the scene from her vantage point, the women below fell silent. And then she addressed them.

'I swear before the sky above and the earth below that I am innocent. I want you all to carry the news when you return to Georgetown and print it in the *Chronicle* and the *Stabroek News*. I know what everybody does call me. But my name is Erzulie.'

The announcement took her escort by surprise and she tried to chivvy her charge along and down the steps. There were strict rules about Shallow-Grave not having contact with the other women. But Shallow-Grave remained composed and she slowly descended the stairs in her own time. When she reached the bottom, she first looked up at the sky and then knelt to kiss the ground before proceeding calmly on her way. She ignored the admonitions of the prison guard at her side. As she passed the other women, the air became fresh with a zingy, salty sort of smell and they could see her lick what looked like grains of salt from her lips.

For Margot, seeing the gleaming statuesque figure on top of the stairs, with the bright blue sky stretching away behind her, was an epiphany. From that moment on, Margot knew that it was through Shallow-Grave that she would find her salvation.

Shallow-Grave's diet proved to be a problem for the authorities. Fish was the main fare in the prison, every sort of fish, fish soup that looked like grey fluff floating in the dish, even fish water to drink. But Shallow-Grave found shrimps and unscaled fish distasteful and pushed anything like that to the side of her plate. Rice-pap and bush tea were acceptable to her. Eventually, because of her commanding presence, some of the warders found themselves sneaking in fruit for her.

All the women in the jail craved fresh fruit and vegetables. Fights broke out in the dormitory over whose turn it was to tend the kitchen garden. Although the produce from the garden was scanty and destined for sale elsewhere, it was sometimes possible to smuggle a piece of callaloo or some peppers which, if not eaten, could be exchanged for tobacco. Every morning the inmates recited the Guyana pledge and sang the national anthem. The ration of water was given out each day. Everyone had a five-pound milk tin to hold the water and it was an art to use it effectively.

To the annoyance of Miss Vinny and the kitchen squad, who were taken to bathe in the stone communal bath after Shallow-Grave had completed her ablutions, it seemed that Shallow-Grave had an inexhaustible supply of water, for the whole bath remained damp and glistening with drips. Miss Vinny would suck her teeth at the sight of it.

Miss Vinny was a sixty-seven-year-old ex-Sunday-school teacher and a murderess in her own right. She was one of the longest-serving prisoners and resented the attention and respect that Shallow-Grave attracted. She scowled and fixed her glasses. Her hair, scraped back and tied with a scrap of cloth, stuck out at the back like the bristles of a yard brush.

'That woman gettin' favours,' grumbled Miss Vinny. 'All this rabble in here. They all criminals,' she confided to some subdued new inmates who had been relieved to find that, although the dormitory windows were barred, the dormitory was reasonably fresh and airy.

With noises and signs, Margot did her best to obtain what information she could about her new idol. At first, she made contact with Shallow-Grave through her enormous shy smile. Later, she proved her devotion by giving Shallow-Grave cigarettes and fruit which she smuggled through the grille of her cell window. Margot thought Shallow-Grave the most devastatingly beautiful and impressive creature she had ever seen. Shallow-Grave received all this attention graciously as if it were her due. Once Margot found the stub of an old candle and passed it through to Shallow-Grave. In this new passion of servitude, Margot felt herself coming alive again. Anything she could find, she delivered to Shallow-Grave, even if it was the bluey-mauve jacaranda petals shed by the tree just outside the wire netting of the prison enclosure.

Shallow-Grave continued to accept this service as if it were rightfully hers. But she sang more often and some miracle cleared Margot's ears of the buffeting winds that normally blew there and enabled her to hear Shallow-Grave's soothing voice:

ERZULIE

> Them that's got shall get,
> Them that don't shall lose.

Margot lay on her bed in a rapture. The matter was sealed as far as she was concerned. From then on she was the devoted servant of Shallow-Grave.

Lock-down time was half-past three. Late one afternoon as dusk began to fall over the prison, an East Indian woman known as 'Catchme Latchmi' who had been found guilty of smuggling a hundred cans of Nestlé's milk into the country, hung on to the bar listening to Shallow-Grave singing:

> If you can't see the one you love,
> Love the one you're with.

Miss Vinny was sitting in a sulk on her bed because the newcomers she had befriended were apparently related to a government minister and Matron had insisted that their beds were to be specially made up with fresh blue sheets and pillows in contrast with the other cots. Miss Vinny had only been mollified by finding a Georgetown telephone number in Margot's kitchen-apron pocket, a number which she intended to use at some time in the future.

Suddenly, Latchmi yelled, 'Miss. Miss. Come quick.'

Through the window, in the dusk, she had spotted a snake undulating swiftly across the courtyard in the direction of the special cells. Soon, one of the warders was hurrying across the yard with a kerosene lamp. When she opened up Shallow-Grave's cell, she was greeted by the sight of Shallow-Grave sitting upright in a pink shortie nightie. It took a few seconds for the warder to realise that Shallow-Grave, still crooning, was caressing the brown-and-yellow paw-paw snake as it twined and wreathed around her neck. The warder, shaking with horror, went to report the matter to her colleagues.

From then on, rumour abounded that Shallow-Grave was, in fact, a water mumma.

When Margot was released, she returned to Georgetown to observe Shallow-Grave's trial. At weekends, unable to bear the separation from her idol, she returned to New Amsterdam. She secured a room in a house in King Street not far from the jail. Margot hoped to be able to catch a glimpse of her idol or smuggle messages to her.

Every Friday, Margot returned to this room. One dark, dingy curtain fluttered at the window. The cupboard on the side was rotting with old woodwork. The bed sheets were patched and greasy with age. The wind brought flecks of grey, cane ash through the window. Tiny weightless flies settled on a pair of the owner's damp panties, pegged up in a corner to dry. Outside the door, in the kitchen, stood a flaking stove with rusted canisters of gas under the sink. But she was happy. On her first Friday, through the window, she saw a man behaving oddly. He was standing on tiptoe at the side of a wooden house that was barely standing upright. His arm, up to the shoulder, was reaching through a hole in the side wall. Margot could not figure out what he was doing. Then she realised he was fishing around to see if he could feel anything worth stealing.

Something had gone wrong with New Amsterdam. After its heyday in the last century, the town was now in full rigor mortis. It was a town with memory loss. Street names had dropped off and not been replaced. The buildings were wooden skeletons, leaning against each other as if they had a headache. By the stelling where the ferry plied its trade across the Berbice River, the rusting hulks of sixteen abandoned buses paraded their dereliction, one still displaying its destination in faded letters – Crabwood Creek.

Discussion in the town revolved around health. Half the population had been afflicted with a mysterious condition which resulted in everyone producing white shit with lacy fronds.

'And what is it when you teeth wobble and bleed in you gums?' asked a man buying a slab of cheesy yellow cake from the bakery.

'Me na know,' replied the proprietor. 'Everybody sick these days. I gat pain an' I vomitin' some stuff yellow like lemon. Somebody done this place someting. De whole place gat a spell on it.'

The conversation turned to crime.

'You hear what happen in New Street? Dey chloroform dem. Dey woke up on de floor. De bed take away from under dem. Everything gone and dey gat dis sweet, strong taste in dey mouth. When dey run for de police, police say dey caan' come 'cos dey don' got money for gas.'

Such stories of a town bewitched ran riot wherever people congregated. One girl came out of her bedroom to find a young woman calmly removing all her clothes from a wardrobe on the landing outside. Another man left a pot of food on the stove for a few minutes and when he returned, the pot of food had been stolen. The town seemed to be in the grip of a nightmare. Worst of all, someone had seen a dog running from the hospital with a package in its mouth.

It stopped by a trench to worry the brown parcel open. A nine-inch, semi-transparent human foetus fell out and the dog ran off triumphantly with the embryonic child in its mouth. In the last year, three young couples had crawled under the raised floor of the Catholic church and taken poison.

Margot sat on the bed and tried to work out how to contact Shallow-Grave.

Miss Vinny enjoyed the position of 'Trusty Prisoner'. She held the privileged and much envied job of cleaning and sweeping out Matron's office once a week. No one knew how she had obtained the private number of Mr and Mrs Armand Jenkins in Georgetown, but every time she went to clean the office, she took the opportunity to use the telephone. She cherished her new-found relationship with Rita Jenkins. Even though it was a rather one-sided friendship, it calmed Miss Vinny. She liked to feel she had a place in the life of the middle classes. It soothed her ego which had to withstand the myriad humiliations of prison life and gave her a satisfying feeling of superiority. The calls, when she could make them, were the highlight of her weekly routine in jail.

'Good morning. I just callin' to find out how you goin' through.' Miss Vinny's face contorted with the effort of producing her best standard English. 'I hope you not findin' the rain too wet.'

She was standing with her back to the doorway, her broom in one hand and the telephone in the other. She did not see Matron enter.

'Put that telephone down immediately.'

Miss Vinny dropped her broom with shock. She hung the telephone back on the receiver without saying another word.

Matron escorted her along the faded wooden corridor back to the dormitory, scolding and threatening dire punishments. Immediately, on reaching the dormitory, Miss Vinny was stripped of her trusty's arm-band.

Miss Vinny did not take well to this new loss of status. She mumbled constantly to herself. She had been taken off duties in the kitchen garden and was similarly denied access to the administrative offices. She was reduced to being an ordinary prisoner. It did not suit her. She began to brood.

And then, one afternoon in the dormitory after lock-down, a strong wind began to blow through the bars and one of the women got up to close the shutters. Miss Vinny, who had been moping on her bed, got up and grabbed the woman's arm to stop her.

'I goin' catch that wind,' she said. 'Long time since the wind ain' catch.' Her voice had a hard edge of determination. The rest of the women in the dormitory hoisted themselves on their elbows and turned to see what was happening.

Miss Vinny strode over to each window in turn, flinging the shutters open. The jail was not far from the wide Berbice River and the blustering Trade Winds blew through the windows. Soon the room was filled with wind. Some of the women started to remonstrate but Miss Vinny, shaking with what seemed like rage, hurled herself like a tornado from one window to another. For a while she stood at the end window, gulping in enormous amounts of air until she started to breathe fast and heavily in panting wheezes.

And then she reeled over to the centre of the room, her arms extended like a child playing aeroplanes. Her foot stamped down in a regular rhythm and her spine arched. Suddenly, Miss Vinny felt released to do something she realised she had wanted to do for a long time. She no longer yearned to speak to that silly woman in Georgetown. She wanted to do something she remembered her Surinamese grandmother teaching her. The Winti Dance. She wanted to do the Winti Dance. She used the beat of her foot to remember the words her grandmother sang:

> *Fodu dede, ma a de*
> *Yu kapu en nanga howru*
> *Ma a de.*

No sooner had she begun to move around the room than her tongue became empowered with a host of sounds, an extraordinary range of noises. Each new one took her by delighted surprise and affected the movements of her body. Each one flung her into a different position to a subtly changed rhythm. She had tapped into a stream of energy. Sometimes the noise turned her into a tall, powerful man with a limp and sometimes into an undulating, hip-winding woman. At the age of sixty-seven, Miss Vinny opened herself up joyously to the whole pantheon of creation.

As she wheeled around in the centre of the dormitory, Savitri, a heavy woman with dark circles under her eyes, who was prone to depression, rose from her bed, moaning and breathing heavily. She and two other women began to writhe on the floor as if they were trying to slough off their skins. They were tended spontaneously by women trying to ensure they did not hurt themselves and then some of these attendants also began to succumb to the spirits.

By the time the warden had summoned help, most of the women in the dormitory were possessed by an intoxicating and exhilarating frenzy. One or two were in a trance. Only the three newcomers huddled together in a corner, crying, unable to join in.

It took five prison wardens to calm the women down. Some fell across their beds in a state of extreme exhaustion, lethargy or sleep. Gradually, the ecstasies subsided and the prisoners dozed or giggled and looked at one another sheepishly until they too fell asleep to the sound of Shallow-Grave's voice singing from her cell. That night, the special escort was taken away from Shallow-Grave's cell in order that as many guards as possible should be available to protect the dormitory from another such outbreak.

Next morning, the resident psychiatrist from the asylum down the road prepared to leave for his weekly visit to the women's jail. He had fled Singapore after some irregularities in his practice were uncovered. As he left he checked the blackboard in the entrance lobby which had the current figures chalked on it:

In-patients – 63
Out-patients – 143
Escaped – 426

He sighed as he walked towards the jail for his weekly surgery. What could he do with old medicines that had lost their potency? He could not even get hold of the latest scientific papers.

When he reached the jail, he was turned away. Everything was in uproar. Shallow-Grave had escaped.

★   ★   ★

It had been Margot's brainwave to organise Shallow-Grave's escape. It was she who had concealed her mistress in the toilets below deck as the rusty ferry ploughed its way across the Berbice River to Rossignol. And it was her brilliant idea to secrete Shallow-Grave in one of the many unused rooms of the house in Main Street where the Jenkinses rented their apartment.

At nights, Margot slipped out and padded along the creaking corridors, over the gleaming wooden floors, past the solid circular staircase, to fetch bowls of water, soft towels and soap for her mistress.

In her concealed room, Shallow-Grave reclined on a single bed covered by the deep-rose silken bedspread which Margot had, many times, washed and ironed. Sometimes it seemed to Margot that the purpose of past actions is only revealed later. She had always washed and ironed that coverlet with particular care without knowing why. Now she understood. She brushed and teased her mistress's black, wiry hair which spread like bladder-wrack seaweed in profusion on the pillow. She massaged her gleaming cheeks, neck and shoulders and Shallow-Grave accepted all these ministrations like an empress.

Beside the bed, the electric fan rolled its head to and fro like a metal sunflower slowly following the sun. Shallow-Grave liked to be kept cool. Margot often bathed her as she lay naked on the bed. She would lift her leg, tenderly washing the private parts that amazed her with their resemblance to a great purple sea-anemone.

Margot slept on the floor between the door and her charge. During the night she would go and purloin what food she could for them both. No one noticed the creaking of her footsteps down the passages at night because the house produced its own creaks and rustles even when there was no one there. They breakfasted on slices of paw-paw, crackers and cheese, whatever she had been able to scavenge. Margot barely allowed her eyes to leave Shallow-Grave's face as they both ate, so hugely did she enjoy Shallow-Grave's pleasure.

Once she took the risk of staying in the kitchen for an extra hour, squeezing the green transparent tears from grapefruit, and brought the juice back on a tray, served in a huge wine goblet with crushed ice from the freezer. Before dawn, Margot carried bowls containing her mistress's shit and golden urine and emptied them down one of the toilets, flushing it with a bucket of water when necessary.

The house provided everything. There was no need to leave the premises and risk discovery. Margot had become adept at showing herself during the day as usual when she was expected for work. At the day's end, she pretended to leave and just waited for an opportunity to slip back into her hiding place.

Mostly, they stayed in the room during the day with the Demerara shutters open. The room was too high for anyone to see in from the path below. When there was a power outage and the electric fan stopped, Margot fanned Shallow-Grave with a fan of dried woven reeds that she had found on the floor above. Cupboards of dark-red crabwood with tiny louvred panels stood against the wall opposite the bed. Set in the middle of these was a dressing-table made of ebony. A crystal necklace hung over the supporting strut of the oval mirror. One day, rummaging in the tiny drawers, Margot found the rim of a cameo brooch with the cameo missing, an unopened cigar, several small rouge boxes and old lipsticks.

Shallow-Grave reclined, smoking the cigar. Margot fastened the crystal necklace round her mistress's neck and delicately rubbed a little rouge in her cheeks then, with increasing confidence, applied some lipstick until Shallow-Grave began to look like a magnificent carnival queen from Rio.

'Soon we shall go to Brazil. On a Thursday,' said Shallow-Grave. Margot nodded solemnly. The idea of Shallow-Grave as a queen pleased her mightily. She began to make extraordinary head-dresses, temporary by their nature, of paw-paw skin and avocado peel and red and yellow peppers, which she glued together with astonishing dexterity, before placing them on her beloved's head. Then she would hold up a silver-backed hand-mirror for Shallow-Grave to admire the result.

When the house was quiet, Margot slipped out and sorted out new clothing for them both. In the organised maelstrom of the house, no one really noticed the vanishing articles, or if they did, they relied on the fact that whatever vanished usually re-appeared later, that there was a floating sequence of possessions, a dance of objects and articles around the house.

One night while she was exploring, Margot went silently to the top floor where she discovered and pocketed a little bottle of perfume, some amber ear-rings and two combs. She procured a tablet of green-apple soap, some shampoo, a box of pale face powder and some brightly coloured plastic hair rollers. Becoming increasingly bold, the devoted servant took to exploring parts of the house she had never seen. She went silently, her heart thudding, through the large rooms where swimming patterns of moonlight shifted across the shining wooden floors. On one of her nocturnal outings, she discovered the gallery.

The gallery had once been used for dances. Slender columns linked by a tracery of fretwork supported a ceiling with a painted cupola. Margot glided through. The massive oak sideboard groaned with the weight of silver platters, dusty and unpolished. Ornately carved wooden footstools were scattered around and unvarnished wooden plant-holders had been placed at intervals against the walls. On a marble-topped table stood a glass tray and on the tray sat soft, transparent, miniature purple-and-orange balls of gelatine, some round, some bell-shaped, and some in the shape of fish, full of tiny globules of scented oil. She sniffed the faint, intriguing odours and then pocketed them for her mistress who loved all sorts of perfumes and scents.

Near the door was a large costume box. From the box she pulled out a long red velvet cloak, coronets and tiaras, lorgnettes, pantaloons and all the other paraphernalia of theatre. As she had anticipated, when she returned to their room Shallow-Grave was delighted with these. Margot wanted to dress her in the velvet cloak, but Shallow-Grave dressed herself in a straw hat and a black silk T-shirt, crimson boxer shorts, and then performed karate figures in slow motion in front of the mirror.

Later she allowed Margot to drape the cloak around her and serve her food from the china Staffordshire plates she had found, richly coloured with pink, black-edged flowers, decorated with deep-blue and apple-green leaves.

Despite the exhausting nature of her vocational servitude, when she slept at night, Margot breathed peacefully, as if at last she had found a consoling mother.

By now Margot had come to love these night-wanderings. She discovered that the door panels leading to the gallery were painted with scenes of lakes surrounded by dark, tropical vegetation. Downstairs in another part of the house, she found an unoccupied bedroom and lay for a while on the canopied bed, feeling as if the mosquito net was the fine sail of a ship, a gauze of voyaging dreams, and she was a queen from Egypt. She examined the carvings on the legs of chairs. She explored every nook and cranny of the building.

During the daytime, in their sequestered room, Margot and Shallow-Grave heard all sorts of fragments of life and snatched conversation from the rest of the house.

They heard Adèle the housekeeper panting up the stairs to tell Rita Jenkins, 'I gat de videos, Mistress Jenkins. I gat *King-Kong, Return of the Dragon, White Nights* and *Kiss of the Spider Woman.*'

And they heard Armand Jenkins on the phone, trying to reassure his daughter in Canada.

'Of course I want to protect the environment, honey. I care about it just as much as you do.' And then they heard him hang up and laugh with a colleague. 'Hell, if she only knew. I daren't tell her I'm flying off to the Brazilian border on Thursday to inspect the possibility of a new site near Kato where we'll cause twice as much damage.'

Sometimes the sweet voice and American rhythms of Stevie Wonder filled the house with 'Part-time Paradise'.

And so it was not surprising that both Margot, whose hearing had fully recovered, and Shallow-Grave overheard the telephone ringing in the Jenkinses' bedroom in the early hours of one August morning.

Armand Jenkins fumbled to reach the noisy instrument in

the dark. Three minutes later he was fully awake, trying to absorb the implications of what he was hearing.

The tailings pond of the mine at Omai – a huge pit into which were piped cyanide liquids, other chemicals and mill wastes – had developed cracks on two sides, two hundred metres across and six metres deep. Three and a half million cubic metres, over three hundred million gallons of dangerous toxic waste were cascading into the Omai River and then rushing in a massive plume down the country's main waterway, the River Essequibo.

Armand Jenkins nearly wet himself with fright. It was possible to conceal most mishaps and leakages at the mine site from the public and the authorities. Omai was far off in the bush. The government could not police it. Normally they could get up to anything. But this news would be impossible to hide.

He switched on the light and swung into action in his nightshirt. Despite the activity around her, Rita Jenkins lay asleep like a beached dolphin. His voice, magnified by panic, was carried upstairs to the house-guests, of whose presence he remained blissfully ignorant, as he phoned the company chairman in Canada.

'We have a major disaster here. I'll cover it up as much as I can, but for god's sake send down the mining engineers who dealt with the company's same problem in South Carolina. Pronto. And I mean pronto as hell,' he yelled down the phone. Rita stirred in her sleep.

Blinking in real panic this time, Armand argued over the phone that, much as he would like to, he could not keep such a massive disaster from the government of Guyana. He had tried that ploy earlier in the year, withholding news of an unauthorised discharge of cyanide for six days. It had not gone down well. He hung up and went and poured himself a neat rum from the cabinet before phoning Cambior's publicity department.

'There's been a catastrophe,' he shouted down the phone.

'You mean an unfortunate incident,' snapped the public relations man in Montreal, who objected to being woken so early.

'Millions of gallons of cyanide waste is pouring into the main river here.'

'You mean there's been a spill. Some seepage.' Even as he came to full consciousness, the yawning man in Montreal tried to instruct Armand in the techniques of damage limitation. 'Just make sure you control, as far as possible, what is said in the papers. We will put out statements here to mollify the shareholders. If there are any commissions of enquiry, try and ensure that lawyers and businessmen sympathetic to us are on board. Oh yes, and try and plug that leak.' The man hung up.

Armand took a deep breath and rang the local newspapers.

A sleepy sub-editor took down the news and perked up as he did so. A big story. Nothing much had happened since Shallow-Grave's escape and they had drawn a complete blank on that. She had just vanished. With some satisfaction, he changed the headline which had been going to read 'A hundred and twenty-nine days to Christmas' and wrote 'Omai mine seepage'.

Margot noticed that her beloved had started to droop. Shallow-Grave said it was merely because she needed to go for a swim. But the day after they overheard Armand on the telephone, her hair lost its healthy spring and her body broke out in a riot of sores that gathered in groups, sent out messengers, erupted in angry outbursts, opened their mouths and yelled. A revolution broke out all over her skin. Margot was horrified. Shallow-Grave explained that a quiet, lengthy bathe in sea or river would do the trick. She also pointed out that it was time for them to leave the house and head for Brazil. They decided it would be safe to leave and fixed next Thursday for their departure.

Adèle, the Jenkinses' housekeeper, was a stout, down-to-earth woman who came from a practical family. Her sister Mary lived at Bartica, downriver from Omai. Mary arrived to stay with Adèle for a few days until the worst of the poison had passed by and the river had had a chance to clean itself. Hundreds of dead fish had been found. The government had organised for doctors to take hair samples from the Amerindian villagers who lived in scattered communities along the banks, to see if any toxic deposits were detectable. Somehow the samples had been lost on the way back. The Amerindians complained of itching and burning of the skin and blistered mouths. They were too poor to take on the Omai company. In fact, they had no idea of the wealth of the Gold Star people. Later, a few of them were given a handful of dollars for the ruin of their lands and livelihoods, paltry compensation that left the chairman and the board laughing behind their hands in wonder at how they had got away with it.

Adèle listened uneasily to what her sister was saying. It was not like Mary to be superstitious in any way, but now she was talking about sightings of a boat lit with candles that had been seen moving upriver through the choppy waters of the Essequibo. It was sinking near to water-level with the weight of eleven women seated round a magnificent African woman in a blue dress trimmed with red. Each acolyte held a flickering candle and they were singing, laughing and chattering around the handsome woman who leaned back in the bows of the boat, trailing her hand in the water.

Having played down the Omai disaster as much as possible, Armand Jenkins said goodbye to a grumpy Rita and flew south to the border town of Lethem to await the small private plane that would fly him on to Kato, the place chosen for the next mining operation. He stood outside the guest-house where he had been obliged to stay overnight in the miserable heat of a stifling cubicle and bleakly surveyed the orange dirt track ahead of him. It opened on to a slightly broader clay road. His skin itched and he wondered if there had been bugs in the guest-house. He surveyed the dismally small adobe houses that stood on either side of the road and one or two half-built concrete ones. He decided to go for a walk. His private plane would not arrive until two in the afternoon.

It had taken three days for the engineers to stem the poisoned torrent from Omai. Armand had done his best to dismiss worries and allay government fears. He had assured them that the mighty river would cleanse itself. What he had not told them was that the toxic cocktail of heavy metals, chemically bound with cyanide, tends to enter the marine environment and latch on to micro-organisms. Arsenic, copper, cadmium, lead, mercury become more poisonous over time. These heavy metals are ingested by fish and invertebrates and then bio-magnify and bio-accumulate. They travel through the food chain and end up in the human consumer.

Armand mopped his face with a handkerchief. He walked past the small houses which seemed deserted apart from a few fowls scratching round. He had done his best for the company. He thought he would take a walk by the creek at the back of the main store of the tiny town. It might be cooler there.

Coming down the road towards him was the figure of a tall black woman who, even to Armand, looked out of place. Silhouetted against the blue sky, she picked her way along the road in high-heeled shoes that made her stumble every now and then. Each time that happened, she paused and stared aggressively up at the huge sky as if to defy savannah country. The frilly pink nylon housecoat that floated over a too-tight shiny green skirt, plus the fact that her head was a multi-coloured bouquet of plastic curlers, made her look like a fugitive from a hair-dressing salon. To one ear she held a small portable radio from which Armand could only hear a buzz. But she must have been able to detect music because she was singing in a melodious voice snatches of 'Your Cheating Heart'. She nodded flirtatiously at Armand before turning off abruptly and teetering down the slope to one of the unfinished concrete houses, where she ducked into the doorway and disappeared.

Armand bought himself a beer at the shop and took it with him as he turned down by a bridge at the back of the store and walked along the side of the creek. After about half an hour's scrambling along the wooded banks, he came to a dead tree that had half fallen in the water, its bare branches sticking up like arthritic fingers. He sat astride the trunk where it leaned out over the water, remembering the days of his boyhood in Canada when he used to go fishing in the great lakes. He finished off his beer and threw the can in the water.

The sound of a woman singing floated towards him. At the same time, Armand saw the woman that he had encountered earlier. She was naked, dipping herself underwater and standing up. Even in the water, she looked enormous. The breasts of this crooning giantess swung in front of her as she rose from the creek and began to wade towards him, the visible parts of her body shining and gleaming, spangled with drops of water. She did not seem to have seen him sitting astride the tree.

Embarrassed at the sight, Armand remained stock still, hoping she would not notice him. A line of red ants had made its way along the branch where he sat. All at once they made their way up his trouser leg and started to bite his genitals with a fury. Unable to contain himself and with an exclamation of pain, Armand wriggled and slipped off the branch into the waters of the creek. He came up spluttering. There was no sign of the woman. The singing had stopped.

He was looking round once more when he felt a crashing blow to the head. Dazed and sickened, he stumbled forward in the water. Just before he went under, another violent blow rendered him unconscious. Margot stood on the bank with a paddle in her hand, panting with the effort of the blows. Shallow-Grave waded forward and put her hands round Armand's neck. She pulled at the weighty body until it faced upwards, still with the head underwater, and she squeezed her two massive thumbs down on the windpipe, holding the head under until there were no more bubbles.

Still humming, Shallow-Grave pulled the body to the side of the creek. Then she set about scraping at the earth with Margot's paddle to make one of the hollows in the ground that were her trademark and namesake. The two women did not exchange a word. Margot helped, bending her brawny shoulders to dig and scrape as best she could, gazing at her beloved mistress with undisguised admiration as she dragged the body towards the depression in the ground and covered it lightly with earth and leaves.

Hardly anyone witnessed two women departing for Brazil. The shorter of the two held a red-and-blue umbrella over the taller one and would hurry to execute the most menial request. They took the boat across the Takatu, the larger woman holding on to her straw hat against the Rupununi winds. At Bonfim, few people paid attention to Margot and Shallow-Grave waiting at the side of the road for the bus to Boa Vista. Eventually it arrived covered in white dust and they squeezed themselves on board, in between passengers with live chickens in bags and sacks of provisions.

The last that was heard of them was a report from Boa Vista. They had taken a small room over an electrical goods store in a street near the market that smelled of goat-dung, dried fish, sarsaparilla and turtle-egg oil as well as the steam of washing. Margot had purchased a tin tub which she carried home on her head and had been seen scouring the market for the herbs to make the '*banho de cheiro*'. The blue bath, as she called it.

On their first night in Brazil, Shallow-Grave luxuriated in the hip bath, blue waters lapping at the sides, that Margot had prepared with rue, rosemary, basil, rose-mallow, white-mallow, marjoram and broom-weed. The oily leaves of rue, both stimulant and narcotic, gave the water its blue colour. A strong smell, bitter and exhilarating, rose up with the steam from the bath, pouring through the holes in the roof and scenting the whole neighbourhood, bewitching it into an unusual and welcome tranquillity.

The aroma, combined with the melodious voice that mingled with the steam and issued from the scabby window on that hypnotically warm evening, stuck in the memories of local people. It was an evening when peace unexpectedly burst over the poorest quarter of Boa Vista. Quarrelsome couples were soothed, fractious babies stopped screaming, shopkeepers refrained from beating the children who begged from their customers. The dwarf woman who washed laundry with manly vigour in the stinking alley outside the electrical goods· store joined in the singing as she scrubbed clothes on the dolly-board.

Margot took a chipped enamel bowl with roses on it and poured the waters between the glistening breasts of her mistress as tenderly as if she were watering a transplanted cucumber. After the bath, Margot gave her a quick rub down with bay rum. That, combined with the blue bath, was supposed to ward off evil-doers.

Most extraordinary of all, the butcher, the meanest man in Boa Vista, smiled and threw bones and meat to the endlessly disappointed, starving dogs that hung around his shop. It was the first time that anyone had seen in him a sentiment close to pity.

Rita Jenkins stood in the front room, the telephone in her hand, her bags packed. There had been no sign of Armand for ten weeks. He had disappeared without trace. Tearfully and surrounded by friends on whom she liberally showered small gifts, Rita had waited for news of her husband. Now her shredded nerves demanded that she return to her daughter in Canada. In her worst moments, she feared that he had gone off with another woman. She was on the phone to her lawyer.

'How long would I have to wait before it could be assumed he was dead?' she asked, with an eye to her future circumstances. 'That long?' she squeaked in disbelief. The lawyer consoled her with the news that she would receive a huge sum in compensation from the company who would look after her well for the rest of her life. Rita sniffed and hung up.

'Go and call me a taxi to the airport,' she ordered Adèle. 'Coming back here has done me no good at all at all.'

PROVENANCE
OF A FACE

They said he was the greatest white-face mime in Europe. His trademarks were a broken top hat, caved in on one side like a bent accordion, and a white vest with one large red diamond on it that dripped blood-red tears. And, of course, a face painted white as the bones of the dead. He had been around for years.

Despite all this, I felt disappointed when my editor at the quarterly *English Theatre* journal asked me to interview him. It felt like demotion.

'He's had it. No one wants to know. Comedians make jokes about mime artists these days. Why do a feature on a man whose career slumped twenty years ago? There's more interesting stuff in any fringe theatre in London.'

Jobs were scarce. It was a trip to Paris. I went.

The interview had been arranged well in advance, but once in Paris I hit difficulties. He was out of town. I left messages with his agent and manager who prevaricated and apologised and finally fixed for me to meet him two days later. 'He has developed a distrust of journalists,' they explained. To appease me they arranged that I should visit him in his private house in the country. A rare favour, apparently.

With two extra days on my hands, I decided to visit the house where this master of silent acting was born. At the start of his career he had worked the streets of Paris. I found the house where his family had lived in La Goutte d'Or, a down-at-heel quarter of the city, huddled at the foot of Montmartre. I asked the concierge if she could let me in. She stood in the doorway of her hutch, one of those old French women who has never left the cobbled streets of the district, an entirely urban creature with permed hair died black, eyes like black pebbles staring hostilely from artificially pencilled brows, drifts of face-powder under her cheekbones and crimson lips. No, she did not remember the artist's family. She shrugged, accepted the tip and gave me the keys to the apartment which was now empty. Half of the block was unoccupied, due to be renovated as upmarket apartments for the wealthy.

I corkscrewed my way up the steep wooden stairs to the top floor. There was not a lot to see, a set of poky rooms with old light fittings, the roses and leaves like everything else painted stark white. I could see no means of heating the place. It struck me then that the chalky white of his face matched exactly the colour of those flaking white-painted attics and garrets of Paris where popular myth has it that so many artists died of consumption.

It was a chill March day. My shoe leather squeaked as I walked over to the window, trying to see what sort of view he would have had as a child. The usual hotch-potch of blue-grey slate tiles, the colour of the city's pigeons, tilted at crazy angles, including a church with two towers like slate helmets punctuated with eyelets. Lead patching and pale zinc gave the Parisian roofscape its unique misty quality as if it had eaten frost. But over the helter-skelter of roofs, it was possible to see, gleaming in the distance above, the white domes of Sacré Coeur. It must have looked to him, as a child, like a celestial vision, hanging there in the blue sky. Perhaps it was the daily sight of one of its towers, dedicated to the bankers who donated their subscriptions after the siege of Paris, which motivated him to escape from his poor surroundings. For now, apparently, he was massively rich.

Kicking my heels in Paris on the second day, I could think of nothing better to do than visit the Musée d'Orsay. I mooched around looking at the wrinkled bronze stockings of Degas' ballet dancer, Van Gogh's self-portrait with the air boiling round him, and the weighty sculptures of Rodin. Eventually, I settled down in the museum café. It is situated behind a huge transparent clock overlooking the street. While I waited for my beetroot-and-endive salad amidst the clatter and chatter of other customers, I looked down at the scene taking place in the street below. A crowd had gathered around a plump, sallow, middle-aged man whose black moustache bristled with dreadful energy. I watched idly.

In drizzling rain, the man was setting up a large blackboard on which was written a lengthy and complicated protest. At his feet, on the wet pavement, slumbered a huge and lugubrious St Bernard dog. Next to the dog was a wicker cage containing several cats. On top of the cage perched a parrot, chained by the leg. By squinting I could read what was written on the blackboard. Translated, it read thus:

CITIZENS! My dog, through no fault of his own, was attacked in Vichy. He was harassed and assaulted. As a result of trying to defend himself he had to go to court. He was fined an outrageous amount in relation to this minor misdemeanour. In an attempt to put right this injustice, I am forced to travel the country from town to town, collecting money to pay the fine. The cats and bird have come along in an act of solidarity to lend their support.

Thank you for your donation. Pierre Souhiez.

The scene tickled me. It reminded me of how much the French relish words, what a voluble and articulate nation they are. In France there is even a government department to maintain the purity of the language. Nowhere else would a street hustler rely on the written word to such an extent. As a journalist I appreciated this and somehow, it made me even more curious about the man I was to interview, who had made his fame and fortune through absolute silence.

On my way back, a light rain still fell. I felt suddenly claustrophobic in the city's cramped streets. There is something secretive about Paris and its doorways, narrow as the slits in young women, opening on to draughty tenement yards. The light of the sky made the city look as though it was living in a bruise. Buildings with tiers of lacy iron balconies piled one upon the other, sagged like ancient, yellowing wedding cakes. I passed one of those antique shops for the bourgeoisie, crammed with tiny, expensive polished tables and stuffed animal heads. It made me shudder. Even the trees of the city were imprisoned by iron frills cemented into the pavement. I dived into the Métro. A light-skinned black woman from the French Caribbean was singing on the platform. She was fat, fortyish and a little tipsy, wearing traditional dress, bodice, puffed sleeves and a long skirt. The song was gentle and sad. '*Adieu, adieu, Martinique*' went the chorus. The warm musty smell of the Métro itself, far from inducing in me the familiar feeling of pleasant nostalgia at re-visiting Paris, made me feel sick. I heard the melancholic roar of an approaching train. Tomorrow at least there would be a chance to escape and visit the countryside.

The following morning I took the train to Argenteuil. He met me at the door and I was surprised to find a relatively young, elfin-faced man in his late forties. His reputation – more or less that of a national institution – and the fact that he was three times married had led me to expect someone older. The other surprise, given the nature of the man's art, was that he talked non-stop in a gravelly smoker's voice, underlining his words with frequent expressive gestures.

He took me on a tour of his home. It was clear that he was inordinately proud of it but I could not help noticing how like a museum it was, or rather a shrine to himself. The rooms and galleries were hung with portraits and photographs of himself commissioned at the height of his fame. Room after room was crammed with *memorabilia*, artefacts collected on numerous tours, gifts from admiring fans or other famous artists, shelves and mantelpieces lined with mementoes from his act, photographs of himself in various poses, portraits and sketches by some of the best artists of the time.

Initially and for many years his reviews were ecstatic. He still spent much time reading them with pleasure. Sometimes he paid for the notices to be blown up and framed. These he hung next to pictures of himself in costume. His success had enabled him to buy this grand house. The gardens were his pride and joy. They had been formally designed by a well-known topiarist and laid out with stone paths and imposingly carved box hedges. Statues of the famous white-face figure in his top hat and white vest with the red diamond stood in almost every alcove and recess. Some were in white stone, some in plaster. The artist clearly enjoyed explaining to me the meaning of each particular pose, its history and significance.

Back in the house I asked some questions:

'Why do you make your face white?'

'Because that way I can be seen from afar. I sometimes play in enormous spaces, an amphitheatre or stadium. It is important that my face is seen. And I like white.'

'Are you a clown?'

'No. I am a mime of the streets.'

'What is a mime?'

'Someone who expresses all there is to express about life without speaking.'

The emotion that he portrayed best was fear. He told me that he had learned this quite by accident in his first theatre engagement. Like many a young and inexperienced performer, he had peered through the central divide of the curtains as the audience waited expectantly for the show to begin. The house lights were still on. He had been so genuinely appalled by the curious stares of the people in the stalls that he became momentarily paralysed and stared back in horror. The audience then broke into an uproar of laughter which only served to frighten him more. It built up until the laughter and the fear became natural partners, the one depending on the other. It was the purity of that emotional relationship between artist and audience, unimpeded by words, that launched his career. From that night on the manager of the theatre insisted that every show begin with him peeping out from behind the curtains. And it was said that this one expression was so powerful that it had made him his name.

When I asked him how this one face could have such an effect, he became suddenly shy and evasive and refused to explain its provenance.

His cousin-in-law managed his financial affairs. Some say that he was responsible for the bankruptcy. For now I discovered that the artist was not nearly as wealthy as he appeared. There was no question of fraudulence or anything of that sort, but, in an attempt to maintain the prestige of his internationally acclaimed cousin, the man had tended to draw up contracts that were far too generous to employees and theatre owners alike. Enormous bills had started to arrive as well as threatening letters from creditors. Having reluctantly sacked his cousin, the mime artist found himself spending more and more time writing letters, either asking for money or explaining why he had not paid it. When he was not writing letters, he was on the telephone trying to persuade the Minister of Culture to fund his performances or let him start up a National School of Mime. He became increasingly enmeshed in a web of words and words had always been inimical to him in some way.

I do not know what sadistic impulse made me show him the review of one New York critic, known for his cruel pen, who claimed that the artist was well past his sell-by date, that he had been churning out the same old act for twenty years: 'If I have to look once more at the Visage of Horror that this second-rate dumb-show merchant hawks around every performance, I shall, perforce, scream. The world no longer wants to see it,' the critic had concluded.

'And what would your answer be to that?' I asked, experiencing the self-importance of a journalist who thinks he is behaving professionally by putting the screws on his victim.

He studied the piece. Too late, I realised that he was hurt to the quick. Within seconds he had extricated himself from the interview, ordered his housekeeper to bring me afternoon tea and told me I would be welcome to stay until my train left in a couple of hours. Unfortunately, he had just remembered a pressing engagement. Goodbye, he said, with a slightly fey and theatrical bow as he disappeared through the door.

I could have kicked myself. There was nothing to do but drink my tea – brought to me by a housekeeper in whose manner I detected the faintest signs of reproach – and wait for my train. After about an hour, I thought I would take a stroll in the gardens before leaving. I walked along the symmetrical maze of pathways and turned into the area where the box hedges contained various statues of the artist. I turned one corner where the hedges were taller than usual. There, in a niche, I came across a motionless top-hatted figure recoiled in an attitude of such horror and with such an expression of fear on his face that my hand flew involuntarily to my mouth for a second before I could recover myself.

I mumbled an apology to my host and hurried on.

My heart was thumping uncontrollably as I went back into the house. It was the man's housekeeper and confidante who explained to me the full story behind the Visage of Horror which had started the artist's career. He was of part-Jewish descent and his uncle had fought with the Russian army of liberation in Germany during the last World War. His uncle had been amongst the first soldiers to reach the concentration camp at Belsen and witness the figures behind the wire-netting. When his uncle had visited them in Paris some years after the end of the war, the artist was still a young boy. His uncle had told the story of his arrival at Belsen and the scenes he had witnessed. The young boy had never forgotten the expression on his uncle's face as he spoke. He had carried the memory of that face and reproduced it throughout his career. Despite his vanity, the housekeeper explained – and she freely admitted that his vanity was all-consuming – what had upset him was not the bad review by the New York critic, but the possibility that the world would wish to forget such a face.

THE MIGRATION
OF GHOSTS

Vincent Dawes brought his Macusi Indian wife, Loretta, to England for the first time to celebrate the wedding of his niece. The Anglican church of St Mary's in the leafy suburb of Chislehurst hosted the wedding. All through the ceremony, Vincent joined lustily in the hymn singing and sometimes broke into a broad smile when he saw someone he recognised. He had not been back to England for ten years since settling in Brazil where he had a smallholding. He and his wife had been married for five years and had a four-year-old son. Although she was not an unkind woman, when Vincent's back was turned Loretta was harsh towards the child. At home her speech was abrupt and made her sound as if she was shouting. The way Vincent spoiled his son shocked her. Every time his father left home on business, the boy would weep unconsolably and Loretta would throw him out of the house to wander amongst the animals, trying to toughen him up a little. Secretly, she rather enjoyed his tears. Such affection between father and son puzzled her and she resented it. Now she stood self-consciously at Vincent's side, a short woman in a navy-blue straw hat, her long black hair tied back with a bobble clip. Her eyes were two black almonds set in a flat bronze face and she was aware of having the darkest complexion in the congregation.

Light from the summer sun appeared in shimmering globules through the top windows of the church. The bride standing at the altar was a gawky beanpole of a girl. During the service she turned her head this way and that. Sometimes a scrawny forearm appeared from its white silk sheath to push back the veil from her face. A few times, she turned her head right round towards the assembled guests, looking either distracted or smiling beatifically, and once looking lost with the eyes of someone drowning. Loretta shivered, reminded of the white grub that inhabits the kokerite seed in her native savannahs. Her mind wandered and she imagined the bride suddenly turning and taking huge masculine steps down the aisle towards the door and then lifting up her skirts and running into the nearby woods like a white capuchin monkey.

Vincent looked down and gave his wife an encouraging grin. He was proud of her and wanted to show her off.

At the reception, Vincent talked eagerly amongst the guests, explaining with enthusiasm what he planned to do in Brazil, showing photographs of his little son. He introduced his wife to friends and relatives. His face had become florid from the tropical climate and his laugh even louder than people remembered from ten years before. If anything, his brown hair had been lightened by the sun. Loretta dreaded greeting each new person she met, but managed to smile, hoping that her awkwardness did not show. Although she spoke English – her mother was a Macusi from the Guyanese side of the Brazilian border – such social occasions were a strain. She could barely hear people's voices through the gabble of conversation.

Later that night Loretta sat stiffly in her new nightdress on the side of the bed as Vincent undressed. They were booked into a cheerless room over the pub where the reception had been held but nothing could quench Vincent's delight at being in England and his desire that his wife should feel the same. He had drunk too much at the reception and was full of sloppy affection.

'How I do love you.' He bent to kiss her forehead. 'How do you like England?' he whispered to Loretta as they slid between white tombstone sheets. The day before he had taken her sightseeing around London. He longed for her to share his enthusiasm.

'There are too many people,' she said. 'And the dogs look fat and overfed as if they don't get enough sex. And there don't seem to be any pregnant women like at home. And why are there so many police? Every five minutes you are going down a road and you see police. You are being watched all the time.'

What had astonished her most was the amount of food in the supermarket. There was more food assembled in one place than she had ever seen before. And after Brazilian television which she only saw very occasionally in Boa Vista, the English television seemed bland and lacking in violence.

'I suppose you're right.' Vincent sighed and breathed wine-laden fumes in her face as he settled her in the crook of his arm. He wanted her to like everything, to share his feelings, even his memories. Her criticisms disappointed him. They only had a few more days in England before travelling on to Prague for a long-weekend visit to his old friends Iveta and Paul. Then they would come back to London briefly before returning to Brazil.

'Iveta is an old childhood friend of mine. I can't wait to see her again.' His thoughts had moved ahead to Prague. 'Because my parents were communists, we always went somewhere in the Eastern bloc for our summer holidays. We stayed in Prague with Iveta's family for several years running. She's my age – married like me – and we've kept in touch on and off. I'm looking forward to seeing her again. I want to talk politics. See what she makes of the new regime.' Suddenly he thought of his son, who had been left behind with his Macusi grandmother, and added, 'I miss young Roberto terribly, don't you?'

'Yes,' said Loretta. She did not know what the Eastern bloc was, but his mention of communists had brought back to her the memory of a young communist who had turned up two months before at their house in Roraima. She remembered how he had appeared, banging frantically at the wooden door of their adobe house, with his pregnant girlfriend, both of them streaked with red dust and grit. There had been a massacre. Armed police and ranchers had shot down some of the Sem Terra, the landless ones, a few hundred yards down the road. Who knows why there should have been a stand-off just there. The laterite track where the murders occurred was an unexceptional place in the middle of nowhere, surrounded by a vast arid expanse of red savannah. The nearest Macusi village, which happened to be where Loretta was raised, was about five miles away. The Sem Terra people had refused to be moved on by the ranchers and had just sat in the road. It was a set-up. The police arrived and, when the Sem Terra still refused to move, they shot eight of them right there on the ground and several more who tried to flee. The young man and his girlfriend escaped by pretending to be dead amongst the other bodies. Eventually they found their way to Vincent's smallholding.

Loretta guessed that the young communist was not more than twenty-two years old, short with a round serious face and spectacles. His brown hair was straight and fell in sickle curves on either side of his face. He had belonged to the Sem Terra for two years. Originally he came from São Paulo. In his hand he grasped a cheaply printed copy of the Communist Manifesto and some other tattered texts with pictures of Lenin on the front. Even in these circumstances, immediately after witnessing a massacre, his description and analysis of the events were illuminated by ideas and sayings gleaned from these books which he studied every night. Loretta listened carefully to what they said. His girlfriend was due to return to São Paulo where she would have the baby and then immediately give it up for adoption so that she could return and fight with the Sem Terra. Nothing, she said, flicking back her long straight hair, we have nothing. *Nada. Nada.* Loretta silently offered them bowls of maté tea. Just then Vincent had come in from building a pig pen, brushing himself down, filling the room with his sympathetic presence. Loretta did not speak. The Sem Terra were not liked by her own Macusi people. They burned the forest and squatted on the land. The Macusi claimed that the land was Indian territory.

Loretta turned her face to the wall. The bed dipped in the middle, pulling her back towards Vincent whose snores sounded like a door steadily creaking. She put her hand out to touch the stippled cream wallpaper next to the bed. It felt cold and damp. The English room smelled stale and unused as if someone had died there a long time ago. It made her nauseous. For a while, in the dark, she tried to figure out what the rectangular shape sticking out of the opposite wall could be, then she realised it must be the washstand. Eventually she slept, dreaming that, instead of the struggle to fetch water from the well, her house in Brazil possessed taps with endlessly running water.

They flew to Prague. Vincent, brimming with energy, was excited to be back in the haunts of his youth. Loretta found the large Embassy Hotel where they stayed oppressive. Breakfast was served between seven and nine in the morning. There was something disheartening about the restaurant's heavy white tablecloths and the plain white dishes of dull fruit, muesli and cornflakes. The waitresses, uniformly thin girls whom the new, thrusting capitalism had taken by surprise, appeared like undernourished shoots from an old climate, and still retained the habit of keeping a discreet distance from foreigners. They blushed when asked for anything and went around in twos for confidence.

Vincent stood next to Loretta inside the restaurant doorway, optimistically looking round for somewhere to sit. He was curious to see what changes had taken place in the country. Immediately he noticed how the restaurant was filling up with sharp-suited German businessmen, there for working breakfasts. Next to where they stood, one such breakfast was already under way. The German entrepreneur, a fair fleshy man, banged his fist on the table heartily and the cutlery jumped. He spoke in English.

'We can build for you five hundred new police stations at an excellent price,' he was saying to an executive of the new Prague government. 'And if you give us that contract, our accounts department will give you the initial estimates for the new Dachau Road for nothing. Of course, we would hope to benefit eventually from the construction contracts for that road . . .' His voice tailed off as he looked around for the pepper and salt to sprinkle over his sausages and tomatoes. As he dashed salt over his food, he stared sideways at his companion. Then he took a white envelope from his jacket pocket and placed it on the table.

'Well, sadly our own Czech accountants are just not up to the job,' replied the Prague official, who had a wispy moustache and looked too thin for his suit. He picked up the envelope full of US dollars that the German colleague had placed by his bowl of yoghurt. 'I think we could safely say that your accounts department in Germany would be the best people to give us any estimates.'

The more enthusiasm Vincent showed about sightseeing, the more silent Loretta became. She began to resent Europe altogether. They visited Prague Castle. Loretta stared unseeingly at the glass exhibition cases and stifled her yawns. The whole business bored her. Soon she was in a sulk. Later they threaded and ducked their way round Kafka's tiny house within the castle precincts.

'Imagine, this is where Kafka must have written *The Castle*,' said Vincent, in awe. 'It's a wonderful book about bureaucracy – or is that *The Trial*? Anyway, I must get them for you. A great writer.'

They stood on Karlov Bridge and looked down on the olive waters of the Vtlava. The wind was cold and made tiny criss-cross herring-bone patterns on the surface of the water. Great clouds moved fast behind the castle on the hill.

'This all doesn't mean too much to me,' Loretta said,

firmly setting herself in opposition to Vincent's enthusiasm. She pulled her coat collar up against the wind.

'Well, it does to me,' expostulated Vincent, irritated by her negative responses. Sometimes her pessimism exasperated him. 'I love it,' he announced defiantly. 'I used to come here as a child with my parents. I thought you would be interested.'

They continued across the bridge in silence, both feeling in the right. In the middle of the bridge stood six young musicians playing traditional Slovakian songs on fiddles and drum. A confident fourteen-year-old boy with wide Slav cheekbones and cropped brown hair, which leaned forward like iron filings under a magnet, led the band on his fiddle. The slender girl singer looked defiant and free as she swayed to the music. A crowd had gathered around them. Loretta was startled by the appearance of one girl in the crowd who looked like an ice princess. Her blonde hair had been dyed almost white; scarlet lipstick slashed across her pale face. She looked to Loretta as if she had been turned upside-down and stuck in a bucket of bleach. Sometimes, the sheer whiteness of northern Europeans disconcerted her.

The drummer, banging his hand-drum, turned in their direction and Loretta caught her breath in astonishment. He was unmistakably a native Indian like her: the same jet-black straight hair, the same brown face and flat features and fat brown eyelids over black pebble eyes. She pulled urgently on Vincent's sleeve.

'Look,' she said, astounded, 'an Amerindian boy.'

Vincent looked.

'You're right,' he said. 'Let me go and ask.' And in one of the gaps between songs he went up to the band, engaging in conversation and animated mime with them as they tried to overcome the barriers of language. Eventually, he returned, laughing and shrugging his shoulders.

'No, apparently he's not Amerindian. He's from Mongolia in what used to be the the USSR. His parents found their way here some years ago. He only speaks a little Czech. But your people are supposed to have come over from Mongolia originally, across the Bering Straits, aren't they? Maybe that's why you look alike.'

'I never heard that,' she said, frowning a little.

The boy with the drum slung over his shoulder looked towards Loretta with curiosity. He nodded acknowledgement and gave a little bow. They faced each other across tens of thousands of years. She smiled back at him. Feeling unexpectedly liberated, Loretta forgot the sulk that had threatened to spoil the morning and walked happily, arm in arm with Vincent, towards Wenceslas Square.

A street vendor had set up a stall. On one side he was selling old Russian army hats. On the other he was selling empty tin cans garlanded with labels that said, in bold red capital letters on a white background: 'THE LAST BREATH OF COMMUNISM'. Loretta picked up one of the tins and looked puzzled.

'It's a joke,' said Vincent. 'It's empty. Just air inside.' He bought one for her and she put it in her bag, laughing.

In the old part of town they came across more people gathered outside a church in a cobbled square. Loretta caught a glimpse of white.

'Another wedding,' she said.

It took them a while to realise that the bride was a transvestite and that it was a mock wedding, a street theatre event. A gangly youth in a white bridal gown pretended reluctance at entering the church. Three burly ushers in formal wedding attire tried to force him in. Every now and then the bride protested in an undisguisedly deep voice and a booted leg lashed out from beneath the lacy dress with the kick of a stallion. The crowd joined in the fun, egging on the bride and cheering. Finally, the bride shook the ushers free and to a scream of approval from the crowd, made a mad dash up the stone steps and into the tall fluted arch of the church entrance.

Loretta had a disturbing sense of *déjà vu*. She seemed to know every detail of what was about to happen. For a few moments, as she walked along, the future merged vividly with the present. As the experience abated, she remembered the wedding in England and how she had imagined the bride turning into a man. It seemed to be coming true. Sometimes she felt she could make the world like that, dreaming it into existence. She frowned with concentration as she walked along. It all reminded her of something else too, a tale told by her mother who, in turn, had been told the story by a visiting Mayonkong trader from Venezuela.

She trailed behind Vincent as he strolled through streets and markets, never looking behind him, enchanted by the old district of Prague. The images of her mother's story unreeled in front of her eyes like a cinema film. First, there was the stone-like egg, from inside which it was possible to hear noises, words, songs, laughter and screaming. The owner of the stone-egg used to stick his head in there when he wanted to sleep because night was in there. The owner was away. Iarakaru the mischief-maker had opened up the stone-egg. All at once everything went dark. Night had burst out of the stone-egg. The mischief-maker, Iarakaru, was terrified. He started running in the dark, not as a man but as a white monkey. He was the grandfather of all white capuchin monkeys. He went running running into the arched trees at the forest entrance.

Loretta emerged from her daze to find that Vincent had stopped in front of a tap-dancer performing to recorded North American music. He danced on top of a circular granite plinth about three feet high. The sun went in abruptly behind a dark scalloped cloud whose edge was lit with silver. To Loretta, everything seemed sinister all of a sudden. The young man tap-dancing wore a top hat, black tailcoat, white tie and white waistcoat. His shiny tap shoes were black. The click of the shoes sounded staccato on the granite. Amber-tinted glasses gave him the sly appearance of a secret policeman.

'Let us go. Let us go.' Loretta tugged once more at Vincent's sleeve. He conceded and amiably moved on through the quiet streets, away from the tourist crowds. The afternoon drew on. They walked through flaking, decrepit stone buildings which still retained some warmth from the sun. Ordinary people went about their business. This is what it will be like when we are gone, thought Loretta, and Prague closes over behind us as if we had never existed. She would be grateful when they left.

As they walked through the crumbling streets, it began to rain, a light drizzle. Suddenly, in the maze of streets, they stumbled across a heavy wooden door in the wall with the words 'Laterna Magica' written on it.

Vincent pushed and the door opened. Together they entered a small empty courtyard. He shut the door behind them. It was quiet. All around, there were murals on the walls, painted in a childlike, slapdash manner. Rotund, naked women rolled in and under the blue waves, an aqueous erotica in pale blues and yellows, gentle and playful. The sight was entirely unexpected. Its mood belonged to a warmer climate. They stood still in the secluded courtyard as if treading water in the warm centre of the city. The heart of Prague, despite the Czech Republic being a land-locked country, seemed to belong to water spirits. A seductively pleasant, light-hearted freedom permeated the space. The tall buildings around on every side must have contained a few offices because, from nearby, a wave of laughter from some secretaries broke over them and one of the women began to sing.

Loretta's tongue began to tingle. She talked animatedly.

'Do you think spirits can migrate?' she asked. 'This reminds me of some of our own water spirits. There is one story about a carnival, a big fête by the river. The young girls are told not to dance with a man wearing a hat. But a charming man in a hat who is a wonderful dancer arrives. He dances with one of the girls. In the morning she is gone. The man was really a river dolphin. He took her back to live under the water and she lived like this.' Loretta gestured to the murals around her.

'I don't think spirits migrate,' said Vincent, giving the topic his full attention. 'Do you remember when I showed you the Tower of London? Well, you don't find the ghost of Anne Boleyn walking around Roraima in Brazil with her head under her arm. In fact, now I think about it, spirits are quite conservative. They stick around the same place.'

'Perhaps you are right,' said Loretta thoughtfully, but all the same, she felt cheerful, as if she had been sent a message by someone from home.

'My god,' yelled Vincent, smacking his forehead as he looked at his watch. 'We have to get back quickly and change or we'll be late for Iveta and Paul.' They had arranged to meet his old friends that evening for dinner.

The couple lived in a cramped apartment in a dilapidated block of flats not far from where Vincent and Loretta were staying. Another man had been invited for dinner as well, an attractive, younger man who worked as a singer and musician in a band. Iveta's husband, Paul, was a middle-ranking accountant whose firm had nearly gone bankrupt since the velvet revolution. He was a shy man with short, colourless hair, who had grown plump since Vincent last saw him. Vincent watched Paul meekly serve spinach, tomatoes and dumplings to the younger man who was clearly having an affair with his wife.

To Vincent's embarrassment, Iveta, now grown excruciatingly thin, her chestnut hair piled up untidily on her head, shared constant jokes with her lover. Despite the presence of guests, they caressed each other with increasing lack of inhibition as the meal progressed. Her husband's pink face shone with misery as the evening wore on.

Loretta occupied herself with the task of eating. It was a relief that none of her hosts seemed to be interested in either her or the continent she came from. The lack of attention made her feel safely invisible.

'Tell me all about the revolution, Iveta,' said Vincent, clapping his hands together and trying to overcome the situation by exuding his usual *bonhomie*.

'Well, we stood in Wenceslas Square for hours and it was freezing,' said Iveta, taking a forkful of spinach and feeding it to the grinning young man. Clearly, she was not interested in the topic.

'But are things better now?' persisted Vincent.

'Oh yes, I suppose so.' She shrugged in a noncommittal way. 'Children don't have to learn Russian in schools any more. And we have McDonald's and Benetton.'

Paul got up to carve more pork. He tried to patch over Iveta's obvious lack of interest in the country's recent history.

'There is a lot of investment coming in. A lot of new building work. My company of accountants is bidding for a contract to do the accounts for a new road they are building. The Dachau Road. We are very hopeful. The trouble is that outsiders are flooding in to set up new businesses. A French and Japanese conglomerate has bought this old apartment block, so we shall have to move. But if my company gets the contract I shall get a rise and perhaps we can move to a better area.'

Paul knew that a move to a better neighbourhood was his one chance of holding on to his wife. He turned to her. Her head was resting on the young musician's shoulder.

'Where would you like to live, darling?'

'Maybe I wouldn't like to be settled any more. Maybe I would like to tour around,' she said with a flirtatious glance at her lover.

Vincent was taken aback by Iveta's cruelty. At the end of the meal, Iveta offered or rather insisted on giving both of them and her musician friend a lift home. As Iveta took the plates into the cupboard of a kitchen, Paul, not wanting his wife to go out, whispered frantically to Vincent, 'Please don't let her. Please don't let her give you a lift.'

They turned down the lift and insisted on walking back, but it was no use. The musician accepted her offer with a sneering smile and the last they saw of her, she was nuzzling up against him in the front seat of the Lada before driving away, leaving Paul in his wretchedness to clear up.

The situation shocked Vincent. Everything had changed since his last visit when Iveta and Paul had been full of warmth and contentment. He and Loretta walked to their hotel with that shameful feeling of relief that couples have after visiting another couple whose marriage is clearly in difficulty. Their own unlikely match did not seem in such bad shape.

But back in England, that sense of partnership evaporated again. The day before they were to return to Brazil, Vincent borrowed his brother's car and took Loretta for a final spin to see London all lit up at night. For reasons she herself did not fully understand, she had reverted to a mood of resistance to these outings. It was wet and after they had driven for more than half an hour in silence, he pulled the car up on the Embankment opposite a floodlit Big Ben and the House of Commons. The river on their left was silvery black like seething tar.

'What's the matter?' he asked in a temper. 'Can't you see that this is beautiful? Good god. I've taken you to London. I've taken you to Prague. Two of the great cities of the world and you don't like any of it?'

He peered up at Big Ben: the recently cleaned structure of stone lace was biscuit-coloured under the floodlights. Then he looked at her in puzzlement. The street lights made her complexion even more bronze and her hair a deeper black. Suddenly, his wife seemed a complete mystery to him. She stared straight ahead at the colours of the traffic lights swimming in the gleaming wet road.

'Well, I love it,' he continued, half blustering, half disappointed. 'I love our home in Brazil too, of course. But I love this as well.'

She watched the traffic lights change colour. Then she spoke:

'Actually, it makes me sick to look at buildings like this when I have to go back to the shacks that people are living in at home. I don't know why we haven't built things like this. It makes me feel ashamed of my own people.'

Immediately, he was sorry.

'Come on then. We'll go.'

'No. Wait a minute. I want to ask you. What do you think happens when you die?'

'Nothing. I don't believe in anything spiritual,' said Vincent. 'What do you think happens?'

'When I die, I expect my spirit will return to my village and hover around there for a bit until it just dissolves.'

'I would like to believe in reincarnation,' sighed Vincent. 'I really wish I had more than one life. I love life. I want to know what is going to happen. I'd come back as anything just to be here – a tree, a stone step, a feather, anything.'

She stared ahead and spoke slowly.

'Life hasn't been too glorious to me. I wouldn't want to have another innings, as you say about your cricket.'

He waited for her to go on but she just looked ahead at the wet road. Traffic hissed past. Spermatozoa of rain wriggled across the windscreen. She shook her head in bewilderment.

'Once is enough for me. When I done, I done. Life

seems so unjust, so unfair. I wouldn't come back as anything.'

Vincent was taken aback by the conviction with which she spoke. Her body seemed to grow heavier, weighted down with defeat.

'Once is enough for me.' She turned and looked him full in the eyes. 'I can't wait for it to be over. Life has been a burden. All my life my own people have been under pressure – struggling. You are good to me, Vincent, and I am a practical person. I know I am better off than most, but sometimes I still dread the mornings. I want the darkness to stay around me. I can't face the light. That damn thrush, I think to myself as the birds start singing. I've been so battered and I've seen such terrible things.'

She rubbed her thumbs nervously against her closed fists.

'I saw a whole family drown once in the Rio Negro when their canoe capsised. I was nine. There was nothing we could do. We stood on the bank and watched. I still have nightmares. Once some soldiers came running down to the beach by the river. They were a distance away and I thought they were playing with some of the girls from our village, but they were raping them and sticking broken bottles in their vaginas. And look at the massacre the other day. It won't be the last. My own village could be next. Well, I suppose we all have to die.'

Vincent started up the engine. This fatalism of hers always unsettled him. He thought vaguely about the collapse of communism. Maybe it did not disappear but just went up and down like a Mexican wave – disappearing in one part of the world and rising up in another. They drove in silence through the deserted West End. Bright neon lights threw shimmering zigzags of colour on to the black wet streets. He wondered about ghosts. Although he enjoyed his life in Brazil, perhaps he would never feel that he understood it properly because he did not know the ghosts. Just as Loretta did not know about Henry VIII or Kafka or Dachau.

They stopped in traffic under the black dripping iron struts of the bridge over Farringdon Road. The inside of the car window had begun to steam up and Loretta reached in her bag for a handkerchief to wipe it. She felt an unfamiliar shape in the bag and pulled out the tin with 'THE LAST BREATH OF COMMUNISM' printed on the label. As she rubbed at the window with her hanky she pondered on what she would do with the tin. If the young communist was still around she would give it to him. But he had probably left by now. Perhaps she would give the tin to her father back in the village. Containers of any sort always proved to be useful out there.

ENGLISH TABLE WUK

'People's princess, my arse. Of course she smile and hold a few people's hand. She ain' gat anything else to do.'

The grainy funeral of Diana, Princess of Wales unfolded in front of four observers, three of whom lounged on a green padded sofa and one in a large bamboo armchair pulled close to the television in order to watch the procession. Slanting zigzag lines regularly fizzed on to the screen, interrupting the picture. Above the solemn tones of the commentator's voice came the occasional clink of ice tinkling in glasses of rum.

'If you ask me the whole thing is a farce,' came one disenchanted male voice. 'Plenty people work all their lives to help the poor. This woman went home every night to a palace, an apartment with twenty-five rooms, or she partied. She could have bought Angola, never mind havin' her picture taken with a few amputees.'

The sitting-room was large and airy. Outside, yellow keskidee birds shrieked and the cacophonous honks of Georgetown traffic floated in through open windows on the back of the warm breeze. The television screen's colour waned into black-and-white as the city's power voltage dropped.

Auntie May, the owner of the house, stood at the back of the room and slapped a last-minute iron down on the pink silk jacket she intended to wear that afternoon for the flight to Miami. She cast a casual look over to the coffin on the gun carriage. A lanky East Indian man in his thirties whose name she could never remember sat in front of the television, his long legs stretched out in front of him. He spoke up.

'Every nation does like a good funeral. Look at us. Our president Cheddi Jagan dies. Half the people din like him but what happens? Everyone flock out in the street weepin' and wailin' to see the body pass. Death changes your mind about people.'

Auntie May was built like two dumplings – a small one placed on top of a larger one. Her bottom wobbled and shimmered in the tight pink skirt as she vigorously manhandled the iron. She wrinkled up her snub nose. It was not good to speak ill of the dead. These visitors to her house did not meet with her approval. They were radicals, friends of her niece, Adriana, who was home from studying sociology at university in England. She endured them for Adriana's sake because she loved her sister's child. Adriana, a slender, intelligent, jet-skinned girl with black corn-row braids and spectacles, sat forward in the armchair with her elbows resting on her knees and her chin in her hands, gazing intently at the screen, trying to analyse what was happening.

'Is it because she was beautiful? A fairy-tale princess for white people or what?' she asked.

'But look, there's plenty black people in the crowd.'

'Everyone would be beautiful if they spent that much money on they looks and wore all that fancy jewellery,' piped up another slow cynical voice from the sofa. 'It was because she lived out her life in the public eye. She became an ikon. A celebrity. She said she hated the publicity but she loved it. It empowered her. We jus' watching the English monarchy re-invent itself. She's part of the process. Why is it people don' see reality? The rich create the poor, then they want extra praise for throwing the poor a few crumbs. At least we are a republic. We might be an ex-colony but at least we managed to leave all that sentimental rubbish and fantasy behind. Let's drink to reality. A republican future and equality.' They all solemnly raised their glasses for the toast.

The conversation batted lightly to and fro, all eyes fixed on the screen except for Auntie May's. She occasionally put down the iron and flurried around on last-minute tasks to do with her flight later that afternoon.

One of the servants appeared in the doorway and addressed Auntie May. Gita was a short woman of about thirty-five who looked fifty. Her high waist barely made an indentation between her breasts and her belly. She wore a faded floral cotton dress and flip-flops. A semi-squint slanted one of her melted liquid eyes inwards towards her nose and her hair was tied back in an untidy bun.

'Excuse me, mistress. I want to leave early this afternoon. I have to do some English Table Wuk. I lef' de fowl curry in de fridge.'

Auntie May looked up from the ironing board.

'All right, Gita, if you must.' She did not know what Gita meant by English Table Wuk but imagined vaguely that it involved embroidering a pretty tablecloth or something of the sort. 'I'll see you when I get back. Please to clean out the back bedrooms for me properly. I'm noticing a lot of dust in there yesterday. Now where did I put that blasted iron?'

'There,' said Gita in her sonorous voice, pointing at the implement hidden behind a bag Auntie May had dumped on the ironing board. 'The iron is lookin' at you.'

No sooner had Auntie May found the iron than the power went down all over the city. Both television and iron ceased to function. Everyone groaned.

'I hate these blackouts.' Auntie May stomped her foot and stood pouting, her hands on her pink-silk-clad hips. Adriana went to switch off the dead television. Her friends yawned, stretched, complained and began to say goodbye. The electricity was unlikely to come back on for several hours. The visitors drifted off into the early afternoon feeling satisfied with themselves. The spectacle of the funeral had filled them with the mild pleasures of righteous indignation and reassured them as to the rectitude and superiority of their own rational politics.

Back in the kitchen, Gita also felt content at having secured permission to leave early. She lifted up the lid of a pan of boiling ham and held it there for Barbara the cook to add a handful of cloves and some mustard. Billows of escaping steam filled the room with a delicious smell from the bubbling pot.

'Please to pass the ladle for me please,' said Barbara, licking her fingers. Barbara and Gita had worked together for nearly five years.

Gita sank down on her hands and knees to find a ladle in one of the tiny louvred cupboards under a sink full of snook fish waiting to be gutted, their scales glittering like sequins beneath blood-stained heads.

'How your father's funeral was?' asked Gita. Gita did not possess a television, nor did she read newspapers. But the solemn music introducing the programme upstairs had reminded her that Barbara's father had been buried at Blairmont the weekend before.

'It was nice. We did sit up and sing hymns and march about. My brother did call out de words.'

'Call out de words,' repeated Gita like a gong as she peered breathlessly into the back of the cupboard. She had the habit of repeating with grim satisfaction the last few words of whatever had just been said.

Barbara went to the meat safe and took out some spare ribs. She placed them on the counter and wiped her hands on her apron, her ebony forehead shining with steam from the pot, steam that had also dampened the tiny coils of her greying hair.

'They say when you goin' die, you does get strong,' she announced, prodding the ham with a fork. Then she set about wrapping the spare ribs in foil.

'You does get strong. Yes. An' your pulse does move,' gasped Gita, straining to reach behind a pile of kitchen utensils. There was a rattling collapse of egg whisks, graters, colanders, aluminium pans, egg poachers and pancake griddles. She pulled out a ladle and handed it to Barbara.

'They say you don' die if somebody lookin' at you,' continued Barbara, savouring a mouthful of broth, allowing her taste buds to measure the saltiness before swallowing it. 'When somebody go away to sleep thinkin' you is all right – is then you die.'

'You must always stay awake if a dead person is in the house,' said Gita, settling down with the grater between

201

her knees to shred coconut. 'There was a woman died in a house near to me. They covered her with a sheet and the other eight people in the house went to sleep. Well, the dead woman rose up, tore a strip off the sheet and made eight knots in the sheet, one for each person. She began to swallow them. Someone woke up in time and stopped her. They pulled the cotton strip from her throat. She had swallowed six. If she had swallowed all, they all would have died. She come alive and when she see they sleepin' – she vex. Since then, at a funeral, some sleep but others must stay awake.'

The shadows from the sapodilla tree outside fell across Gita's face as she scooped piles of grated coconut on to the draining-board. Then the sun went in and a brief but fierce shower sent spikes of rain lancing through the kitchen windows. The two women peered through the window as they heard a taxi slooshing through the rain to pull up at the gate.

'Mistress. Your taxi come,' Gita called up the stairs from the kitchen door and then flip-flopped back to the window. 'The rain does not want her to go to Miami today,' she remarked ominously to Barbara while watching with the utmost care, making sure that she observed Auntie May's departure with her own eyes. Auntie May left as usual in a fluster of shouted instructions to her staff, farewells to Adriana and angry jabs at the rain with her umbrella. The guard dogs barked fiercely as she hauled her plump legs into the car which sped off almost immediately.

It was already past the time when Barbara should have finished work for the day. She only worked in the mornings. Once the fish in the sink had been packed into the freezer and the boiled ham placed in the fridge, she put on her raincoat, said goodbye to Gita and thankfully let herself out through the gate.

It was what she had been waiting for. Gita had the kitchen to herself.

Ten minutes later, when Adriana wandered downstairs to fetch herself another glass of plum juice from the fridge, she was stopped in her tracks by the sight of Gita's furtive movements through the kitchen door. As she watched, she saw Gita hastily taking all Auntie May's antique silver knives and forks from the drawer and bundling them up in napkins. These she was placing in a large canvas bag alongside two clearly visible silver jugs and some silver tankards and a silver candelabra. Then she took down some of Auntie May's best Royal Doulton china from its place on the sideboard, wrapped each item carefully in more white napkins and placed them, one after the other, in a capacious nylon bag decorated with a Union Jack.

Adriana recoiled from the door post, unsure of what to do. It already preyed on her conscience that she came from a family which employed servants. None of her student friends in England approved of that, however much she tried to explain that it was commonplace amongst middle-class Guyanese. But she knew that even her friends at home in Georgetown would probably support Gita in this act of theft. All property is theft, they would say. Gita is just redistributing wealth. Gita is poor. Your aunt is rich. Gita is redressing the balance. Adriana stepped quietly away from the door and began to climb hesitantly back up the stairs, pretending to have seen nothing. From the stairs she caught another glimpse of Gita methodically securing the bulging bags full of her aunt's beloved silver and crockery. Adriana hovered on the stairs. She felt sorry for Auntie May and responsible for the about-to-disappear valuables. She decided at least to follow Gita and see what she did with the stolen property. Perhaps she could recover it later.

After ten minutes, Gita left the house and set off with a heavy bag in each hand. She threaded her way round gleaming puddles in the road. A tiara of glittering water surrounded the corner rum shop as the sun blazed down again after the shower. The bags contained much of the silverware of the house, wrapped in linen napkins lest it clanked and gave her away. Adriana followed at a distance behind Gita's short, determined figure as she made her way along the streets to where the mini-buses assembled touting for custom. There she put the bags down on the muddied ground amongst the teeming throng waiting for transportation. Adriana, fearful of losing her quarry in the milling crowd, took a deep breath and decided to confront her.

'Gita! What do you think you are doing?' The question came out breathlessly.

Gita spun round in horror at the sound of Adriana's voice. Then she began to laugh right in Adriana's face. The laughter was a high-pitched screech of embarrassment.

'I goin' to Mahaica for the English Table Wuk, Miss Adriana. I bring back everythin' belongin' to your aunt tomorrow. Don' worry at all at all.'

'Well, I think you should bring everything back right now and I'll say no more about it.' Adriana adjusted her spectacles on her nose, a nervous habit, and tried to appear both firm and sympathetic as the crowd jostled around them.

'No more about it,' repeated Gita in some distress, and

then shook her head vehemently. 'No, no, no. You don' understand. Come with me, nuh. Come with me and you will see.' Gita seized Adriana's arm in a powerful grip. 'Come with me. I show you someting,' she insisted, letting go of Adriana's arm for a moment to hoist the weighty bags on to the bus destined for Mahaica. Then she grabbed Adriana's arm again. Adriana weakened and allowed herself to be dragged on to the crowded mini-bus. Gita sat next to her in silence clutching the two laden bags on her lap. Occasionally she coughed and looked out of the window. Every time Adriana asked for an explanation, Gita came back at her with, 'You goin' see in a minute.'

As soon as they stepped off the bus on to the ground, Adriana recognised the yellow, concave face of Abdul the night watchman at her aunt's house. She wondered anxiously whether she had fallen amongst a gang of thieves. Abdul stood looking around him, apparently waiting for Gita with a group of five or six others, some of whom, Adriana gathered, worked in the nearby village of Mosquito Hall. Gita gave them no explanation as to why Adriana was with her and nobody enquired. Abdul merely looked serious, nodded his head in her direction and said good afternoon. After brief greetings, they all set off in silence down the muddy red track of road fringed with bush still dripping from the rains. Adriana tried not to feel uneasy at the fact that they were heading out of town, away from the crowds.

Some twenty minutes later they reached their destination. It was a patch of land, half-hidden from the road by bushes, in front of a coconut grove which had once been an orange plantation. On the opposite side of the road was the burial ground. It had stopped raining. Six men were already on the open piece of land, struggling under the hot sun to manoeuvre a solid mahogany table over the lumpen clods of earth which rain had turned to sticky red clay. They were attempting to place the table as closely as possible to the centre of the field. Two women unpacked a large, dazzling, white damask tablecloth from an Air Canada travel bag. This they arranged carefully on the table, pulling at the edges until it fell evenly on all sides.

By the time Gita and the others had clambered over the field to join them, the table stood slightly unevenly in front of the coconut trees, covered by the tablecloth. The small group of new arrivals stood chatting for a while in the tattered shadows of the stunted palms. The shining coconut leaves moved in the breeze like green plastic flails. Dried grass and clay-soil stuck to Adriana's shoes. She stood and watched, mystified, as the others continued with the business in hand.

Under the open sky, they struggled to set ten chairs in place, four on each side of the table and one at each end. Baskets of food were unpacked. Gita laid out the silverware that glinted in the sunshine. Pride of place in the centre of the table was given to a rich dark plum fruit-cake with plenty of whisky in it, resplendent on its tall, silver-plated cake-stand. Gita carefully placed Auntie May's silver candelabras on either side of it. Gradually, the long table was laid as if for a Victorian high tea. Plates of hard biscuits, every sort of sandwich, cucumber and tomato salads, dishes of preserves, relish, plums, prunes, stewed apricots, silver teapots, decorated plates of Staffordshire china, Royal Doulton china, silver milk-jugs, silver tankards, all crowded on to the table. The wealth of the display was in the greatest possible contrast to the appearance of the people who carried out the tasks, each one of whom was poorly dressed in faded, skimpy, stained and ill-fitting clothes and cheap shoes. Everyone worked quickly because flies and marabunta hornets were already inviting themselves to the feast.

When it was finished and the table, aslant under the afternoon sun, was heaped with food, the group stood back to admire their handiwork. Then they each selected a chair and stood behind it and Adriana heard the words of what sounded like a hymn being sung, accompanied by a drum. The voices, some shrill and some deep, were raised together in an unpractised chorus which petered out towards the end.

'That will make the ones that does bury round here feel nice,' said Gita, mopping her brow and re-tying her headscarf as she came back to where Adriana waited.

'I hope it does keep the Scottish doctor happy,' added one of the other women doubtfully. 'His jumbie supposed to rise up from the burial ground and inject passers-by. If you see him you must cut a hank of 'e hair and tie it to a cabbage palm.' She frowned blindly into the sun.

The group looked back with pride at the fine display. There was a palpable feeling of satisfaction amongst them as they abandoned the laden table to its fate and made their way back to the road across the lumpen field, fixing the arrangements as to who would collect up the dishes and silverware next day. Then they said their goodbyes and made their way down the still muddy road.

As the rest of the group dispersed, Gita and Adriana waited at the roadside, hoping to hitch a lift back to where they could catch a mini-bus. Black clouds fringed with opal light threatened rain again. After a while, the sun set behind the trees, making the whole coconut grove look as if it were suddenly engulfed in a fiery orange blaze. The table stood on its own beneath the lengthening shadows of the trees. A pyramid of mosquitoes danced over the cake. Gradually, the uproar of sunset subsided and slid below the horizon leaving only the white tablecloth to glimmer in the darkness.

Gita finally explained.

'Every year we does conduct a ceremony in order to appease the spirits of the English dead who bury across de road right here. We does leave de table piled with food for dem jus' so. Whoever arrive first in the morning gathers together de crockery and silverware. It is always de same story. Nothing ever stolen. Silverware, dishes and tablecloth always remain intact, jus' how we leave dem. But de food has always been attacked, gnawed and scattered, whether by animals or ravenous English spirits we ain' too sure. Abdul will bring back your aunt's property early tomorrow. It will be safe. That is de English Table Wuk. You see it now?'

Adriana absorbed the information in silence. Bats began to flit overhead. The two of them waited by the unkempt burial ground, the remnants of old tombstones sticking up like broken teeth planted in the ground. Adriana leaned over to try and decipher the names on one or two of the stones. She made out some English names and one Dutch family grave.

After about a quarter of an hour, the headlights of a car approached them slowly along the rutted road in the dusk. The driver stopped to pick them up.

As they climbed into the vehicle, Adriana enquired curiously, 'But what about the Dutch people buried nearby? I saw a Dutch grave. Is nothing ever done for them?'

Gita looked at Adriana in amazement and laughed a

scornful laugh as she folded the empty bags on her lap, holding on to the open window as the car set off again down the uneven road.

'You head ain' good or what? Everybody knows that the spirits of the Dutch are unappeasable.' The car took off, leaving behind the table, a faint glimmer in the night.

A NOTE ON THE AUTHOR

Pauline Melville's first book, *Shape-shifter*, a
collection of short stories, won the *Guardian*
Fiction Prize, the Macmillan Silver Pen Award and
the Commonwealth Writers' Prize for best first
book. Her novel, *The Ventriloquist's Tale*, won the
Whitbread First Novel Award and is published as a
Bloomsbury Paperback.